D1094341

Dead To Me

Dead To Me

Cristy Watson

James Lorimer & Company Ltd., Publishers
Toronto

Copyright © by Cristy Watson
First published in Canada in 2016.
First published in the United States in 2017.

All rights reserved. No part of this book may be reproduced or transmitted in any form or by any means, electronic or mechanical, including photocopying, or by any information storage or retrieval system, without permission in writing from the publisher.

James Lorimer & Company Ltd., Publishers acknowledges the support of the Ontario Arts Council (OAC), an agency of the Government of Ontario, which in 2015-16 funded 1,676 individual artists and 1,125 organizations in 209 communities across Ontario for a total of $50.5 million. We acknowledge the support of the Canada Council for the Arts, which last year invested $153 million to bring the arts to Canadians throughout the country. This project has been made possible in part by the Government of Canada and with the support of the Ontario Media Development Corporation.

Cover design: Tyler Cleroux
Cover image: Shutterstock

978-1-4594-1160-9
eBook also available 978-1-4594-1158-6

Cataloguing data available from Library and Archives Canada.

Published by:
James Lorimer & Company Ltd.,
Publishers
117 Peter Street, Suite 304
Toronto, ON, Canada
M5V 0M3
www.lorimer.ca

Distributed by:
Lerner Publishing Services
1251 Washington Ave N
Minneapolis, MN, USA
55401
www.lernerbooks.com

Printed and bound in Canada.
Manufactured by Friesens Corporation in Altona, Manitoba, Canada in December 2016.
Job #228979

This book is dedicated to my sister, who has supported me in so many ways over the years, but especially these last few. Elisa, I finally wrote a book that has appeal for you! And as always, it is also dedicated to the youth who struggle with anger and finding their way — you inspire me every day!

"Run, run, as fast as you can."

Prologue

The buzzer rang. Mom called out to tell me Uncle Gerry was on his way up. I ran to open the apartment door and watched as he sauntered down the hall. He was wearing his crazy fishing hat, even though he never fished a day in his life. Fishing had been my dad's thing.

"Happy birthday, *Mi hijo*," Uncle Gerry said, as he stood in the doorway. He always called me that, Spanish for *kid*. "Ready to go have some fun?" he asked. Uncle Gerry wanted to make the day all about me. It was my twelfth birthday, so I planned on having a good time!

I waved bye to my mom and settled into the car. On the drive out to Harrison Lake, he offered me a chocolate bar. Then he popped a huge wad of gum into his mouth and blew bubbles at me. I laughed while we flew down the highway. Out the side mirror I could see our boat hitched behind us, moving in sync with the car.

As always, I slept almost the whole way. As fast as Uncle Gerry drove, it was still an hour and a half from our apartment in White Rock to the lake.

"We're here, *Mi hijo*," he finally said, tousling my hair. He never called me Logan and I was good with that. Usually we launched from Killer's Cove, but this time Uncle Gerry decided to launch from Sasquatch Park.

It took about twenty minutes to ready the

boat. Then Uncle Gerry started the outboard engine. Turning the craft toward the centre of the lake, he bellowed over the rumble, "Turn it up!" And as he cranked the throttle forward to full speed, I blasted our favourite tune. "Highway to Hell" blared across the water, echoing back to us.

"Okay," said Uncle Gerry. We'd been screaming across the lake for ten minutes. "I think we're far enough away from the other boats. Your turn at the wheel."

For the next half hour, I laughed like a wild thing. The wind whipped my hair back and made my eyes water. As the boat bumped up and down over the waves, Uncle Gerry put his arm around my shoulder. I felt like my dad was close by.

"It's kind of cold out. I wish it was summer," I said. I felt a shiver run down my shoulders. It was late May and there were only five weeks left of school until summer break.

"So do I, *Mi hijo*," said Uncle Gerry. "We

Mexicans need sunshine, and loads of it!" I'm only half Mexican, but I figured I needed just as much sunshine as my uncle. Maybe even more! He stopped the boat in between the Hot Springs and Echo Island. Then he pulled out a twelve-pack of Corona and popped the caps off of two bottles.

"A birthday surprise for you," he said. And he handed me one of the bottles. He guzzled his drink.

I held the beer, figuring he would ask for it when he was ready.

"We have a tradition in the Gomez family," Uncle Gerry said. He grinned and swigged more of his drink. The bottle was almost empty. "It's something we do out on the lake. Did you know that your dad was twelve when your grandpa gave him his first drink?"

I shook my head.

"Well, I was twelve when your dad snuck booze from your grandpa's stash and gave *me* a beer. Your grandma never caught on. And if we keep this secret between us, your mom won't know either."

I wasn't sure he was serious. Was he really giving me a beer? He popped open another beer and tilted his head back to drink. He nodded for me to start mine. I put the bottle to my lips and let the cold liquid roll down my throat. It was kind of bitter, and I burped after three gulps. I watched Uncle Gerry and took swigs in time with his drinking. Before I knew it, my bottle was empty and my head was spinning.

"You aren't supposed to knock it back like Kool-Aid," Uncle Gerry laughed. But he was on his third beer, and I wanted to live up to the family tradition.

In no time, he'd finished five bottles. While he swigged his beer, we drifted on the lake. We watched the other boats pass by. We watched eagles fly overhead. We talked about hundred-year-old sturgeons.

After his seventh bottle of beer, Uncle

Gerry's mouth got loose. He began talking about what happened the day he and my dad were out on the lake, eleven years before.

"We were having one hell of a good time, your dad and me. Laughing like fools. It was your dad's twenty-fifth birthday. Five years older than me. I remember being jealous because he had it so good. A great job at the bank and the prettiest wife in the neighbourhood." He smiled and looked across the lake as though he could see the memory.

"He sure was proud of you," Uncle Gerry continued. "You were just a year old — cute as anything." He leaned over and squeezed my shoulder. "He'd be proud of you still." He choked on the last words and went back to the cooler. After he cracked open another beer and passed me one, he patted my knee. He looked at the rolling waves and sighed. I could smell the beer on his breath.

Hearing Uncle Gerry's memories gave me a weird feeling and my knee began to shake.

Uncle Gerry moved his hand to the rim on the side of the boat. He peered over the edge, and then sighed again. "No way to say it, but to plunge right in. Your dad and I had been boozing all day — celebrating his birthday. I remember watching him lean over the rail. And you know how I love a good gag?"

He turned back toward me but didn't meet my eyes. He kept his head bowed. "I swerved the boat back and forth across the lake. I watched your dad sway and stumble. It was funny to think of the fisherman being the one losing his balance."

Then his voice got so low, I had to strain to hear him.

"How was I to know there was a deadhead bobbing in front of the boat?"

Chapter 1

Suspended

Four years later

It's the first week of March and only ten days to Spring Break. I'm strolling the halls between classes, thinking about how in a few days I'll have loads of time for cruising with Cisco. It's murder when we go out on a weeknight, because I can hardly keep my eyes open the next day at school. Cisco doesn't have to worry about that, since he graduated last year.

As I pass a group of guys that constantly

get on my case, I overhear one of them mumbling to the other jerks, "That's the dude I've been telling you about. I think he's part of a gang. You know, the guys we call *border hoppers.*"

In seconds, adrenaline fires into my fingers. I turn and feel my hands shove the guy, hard. He falls back into the locker. "*Cabron!*" I yell, using the Mexican swear word Uncle Gerry taught me years ago. Before any of his buddies can move, I have the guy in a headlock. I'm ready to give him a smackdown when the principal appears.

"Logan Gomez! My office — *now!*"

I clip the jerk anyway as Mr. Williamson knocks my arm down.

"They started it!" I shout, my body still in overdrive.

The principal marches down the hallway, his huge steps matching his tall frame. I shuffle behind him, trying to think of what to say when we reach his office. Students loitering in the hall snicker as I pass by them. They have seen this sight too many times.

"Mr. Gomez," he begins, motioning for me to sit in a broken chair. His office door closes with a thud behind me. "I'm calling your mother — you're suspended."

"Don't you want to hear my side? How those jerks are constantly on me? How they're racist?"

"I didn't see you talking it out with them. All I saw was *physical* contact — from *you*. That's an offence at our school. Clear and simple."

Yeah. He sees what he wants to see, clear and simple.

He dials Mom at work. She'll be pissed now!

"Mrs. Gomez? Yes, it's Mr. Williamson, Logan's principal. Yes, I know. I'm sorry to bother you at work again . . ."

Ever since I started at this school, I've been harassed by assholes. I was pretty scrawny when I entered high school in grade eight. I remember the first time I was bullied. It was the second week of classes and I had a dark summer tan. I looked like my dad's side of the family — totally Mexican. So these creeps were giving me attitude. A Grade Eleven guy was walking by. He stepped in to save my ass. That was the first time I met Cisco. Like my dad, he's from Mexico, and he's been looking out for me ever since.

"Thank you, Mrs. Gomez," the principal's voice cuts through my thoughts. "I'll have Logan wait in the hall for your arrival. We'll talk about his re-entry at that time."

I plunk down in my usual seat in the hall. Every passing student gives me the eye. I push my hoodie back from my face and return their stares. As I wait for my mom, I think about calling Cisco and going for a ride. That would take the edge off things. Maybe a few beers first, so I have a good buzz. And then I'll call Quinn, who's been my best friend since we were little kids. Maybe he'll join us this time, even though he's always telling me Cisco is bad news.

I'm almost asleep by the time Mom arrives. She talks with Mr. Williamson. Then I follow her all the way down the hall and out to our car. I only half listen to her rant about how the time she spends away from her job will be deducted from her pay. I've heard it all before.

"Logan, I don't know what to do anymore," Mom says as she plops down in the driver's seat of our old Honda. "I've called your Uncle Geraldo. He wants to come speak with you. Maybe he can help you sort out what's going on."

As I slam my door, my voice rises. "Why the hell would I want to talk to him? He's been dead to me for four years."

"Because I see you sliding down the wrong path. You're so angry all the time. I hardly recognize you anymore."

"Yeah? Well, maybe that's a good thing. At

least I'm not like Uncle Gerry. I have nothing to say to him. And I doubt he has anything to say to me."

"I think he has plenty to say, if you'd just give him a chance."

We drive the next few blocks in silence. Then Mom turns the car into the driveway of our apartment block.

"He wants you to join him for the Cinco de Mayo Celebration. The one on Commercial Drive in Vancouver. Wouldn't that be fun? It would keep you connected with your dad's heritage and . . ."

As Mom pulls into the underground parking lot, I don't wait to hear the rest of her sentence. I jump from the car and run to the door. I take the stairs two at a time to our floor. Once in our apartment, I slam into my bedroom and flop face-first onto my bed.

Several minutes later, Mom walks into my room, ignoring the closed door. She sits by my desk and talks to the back of my head.

"Logan, I wish you'd give your Uncle Geraldo a chance. You used to love seeing him." I don't respond but my body tenses. "I don't think I've told you this before," Mom continues, "After your twelfth birthday, your uncle wanted to make sure you were safe. He stopped drinking that day. He hasn't touched a drop since then."

"Well, good for him! Too bad he didn't stop drinking *fifteen* years ago!" I bury my head in my pillow. I can hear Mom mumbling, so I pull the pillow tighter around my ears. After a long silence, I lift my head in time to hear my bedroom door close.

I slam the wall with my fist. After a few minutes, I grab my key fob and head to our storage locker. It's just past the laundry room in the basement of our building.

It's dusty in the storage room, and I hear mice scrambling in the corners. I unlock number 225, where I stash my booze. I swig three huge gulps of vodka. Then I tighten the lid on the bottle and place it back inside the suitcase. As the liquid travels through me, I feel a calm filter into my body. Now I can face the rest of the day.

Chapter 2

Surprise Date

It's my first day back at school after my suspension and I'm heading down the hall. The usual suspects are hanging around their lockers. I know they'll push my buttons because I have unfinished business with them. But another suspension will get me expelled. I don't want to risk that over these assholes. I detour down the hall that connects to the library. I hardly ever walk this way.

By the door to the library there are four

girls in a huddle. They look like they are the same age as me, but I can tell from their smartphones and clothes that they have money. As they point at me I'm able to catch a few of their whispered words. They are saying something about a 'gang' and 'he's trouble'. I even catch the word 'dare'.

As I saunter toward them, I figure if one of them is going to take up the dare, I hope it's the totally hot one. Her long dark hair rolls over her shoulders and down her back as she leans in to whisper with her friends. Then she looks up at me. She smiles as I get close. My feet stop in front of her and I grin back.

"Kayleigh," she says and steps closer to me.

"Logan," I reply, and move within inches of her face. Her breath is warm and heats my whole body. As the bell rings, her friends tug at her sleeve and tell her it's time to go. She stays put and keeps her eyes locked with mine. I do the same.

Soon the halls are empty except for loose

papers, a tattered binder and a sad, grey jacket someone has left behind.

"I wasn't into first block today, anyway," I say. "How about you?"

She hesitates for a moment, and looks down the hall. A teacher pops his head out of the classroom closest to us, and Kayleigh drops her eyes. As the door closes, she grabs my hand and hustles us toward the school entrance that opens onto the field. We set off for the wooded area beyond the school.

We barely make it into the trees before our mouths lock. Kayleigh leans back against the trunk of an old cedar. She has one leg raised slightly. I lean into her body, our tongues linked. I don't know how long we kiss, but when we finally come up for air, my first words are, "I'm starving! Let's get some food." She giggles. "I'm buying," I add.

Instead of McDonald's, I steer us toward the Taco Del Mar. "I'm having a burrito, how about you?" I fish money out of my pocket as we approach the counter.

"Taco salad, I guess?"

We fill our cups with pop and grab a seat. While we wait for our order, Kayleigh bites her lower lip. "Crap. If my folks find out I skipped Pre-Calculus . . ." she slurps her drink.

I place my hand over hers. "You can make up one class — it's no big deal."

"Have you taken Mr. Tomlinson's Calc? It's brutal."

I should admit I don't know how tough it is. I'm taking lower-level math — Workplace and Apprenticeship. But I don't say anything as she lets her hand slip away from mine to grab our food tray.

I chow down on my food, but Kayleigh only eats the lettuce leaves in her salad. "I don't know what just happened," she says, smiling. "I got caught up in your dangerous good looks. My folks are going to kill me." She strums the table with her fingers. I pick at the meat in her salad, since I've already finished my meal.

"They don't have to know you skipped."

"Yeah, but I have a test this week and I am so totally freaked over the lesson. I have to pass this stupid course to get into UBC."

"Jeez, it's only grade ten. You've got loads of time to figure things out."

She looks up, her eyebrows raised. "You haven't met my dad. He has crazy high standards that no one can live up to. I can see the look on his face if I brought you home. You are . . . so not what he would expect." A grin curls the corners of her lips and she gets a glint in her eyes.

I've had a few girlfriends, but mostly ones from my apartment building. Rich girls usually avoid guys like me. But Kayleigh is clearly into me. Maybe my being a "bad boy" has something to do with it. I can't deny that she's hot.

"Do you like motorcycles?" I ask.

"Totally! Do you have one?"

"Not yet. But I'll be saving up for one

soon," I say, trying to sound cool. In reality there's no way I could afford a bike. My part-time job at Zellers covers my cell phone and not much else. "I go with my buddy Cisco, sometimes. He has a great ride."

I realize I need to make plans to see her again. "Maybe this weekend you and I could head to the car and boat show? We can check out the newest models." I think of her arms wrapped around my waist as we sit on a Yamaha R1.

"Sounds like fun," she replies. Then she looks at her watch. "Damn, I hate to stop our good time, but I better get back to school for next block. If we want to hang out this weekend, I can't give my dad any excuses to ground me, right?"

"I guess." I'm not ready to leave the restaurant. I look at our reflection in the window. My hair is just as black as Kayleigh's. Her skin is the colour of cream, contrasting with the dark tone of mine. But one thing is for sure — we've got to be the best looking couple in our high school.

✳✳✳

On the weekend, I pick Kayleigh up at her house. It's a monstrous, two-storey home that fills the whole lot. Since it's pouring rain, I have my hoodie up.

I'm expecting her to answer the door after I ring the bell. But it whips open and a man who must be her dad is standing there with his arms crossed. It's already a cool morning, but the icy stare he gives me seems to drop the temperature twenty degrees. I watch as he takes in my runners with holes in them, and my tattered jeans. I want to tell him I dress like this on purpose, not because I can't afford better clothes.

Kayleigh is in behind him, trying to get around to the door.

"Not so fast," he barks.

"Dad, we're going to miss the bus. I'm not waiting half an hour for the next one."

He motions for me to come in and points toward the living room. "You," he says, addressing me. "Wait there."

"But, Dad!" Kayleigh is clearly anxious to get out of the house. I can hear them arguing in the hall.

"He's dressed like a hood," her dad snaps. "Surrey has had a recent spike in crimes from several groups of youth, including his type. What are you thinking?"

Before I hear Kayleigh's answer, my fists curl. I could knock that fancy vase off its perch on the shelf beside me. But I control myself.

"I'm thinking," says Kayleigh in a loud voice, "that you don't get to decide who I see or like. That's my decision."

"As long as you live under my roof and I pay your bills, I have a say. And I don't want you getting involved with someone in a gang."

I have to laugh. Cisco and his dudes aren't

affiliated. They like partying and street racing, but they aren't in any gang. I let my hands relax and step toward the hall. Kayleigh's dad glares at me.

"You don't know me and you don't know anything about Logan," Kayleigh says angrily. She grabs my hand and yanks me forward. Together we storm past her dad. I look back as we hit the sidewalk to see him shake his head. He slams the door on his way back inside the house.

Once on the bus, Kayleigh sits beside me and leans her head against my shoulder. We stay that way for the whole ride to the show.

Chapter 3

Fast Ride

"Sweet!" I holler out the open window. I'm in the front passenger seat of Cisco's car. Quinn and one of Cisco's buddies are in the back seat. Quinn's watching out the tinted side window and I'm focused on the route ahead. Cisco's Crown Victoria screams down the road away from the city.

I reach out in front of me for the dashboard as Cisco slams the brakes. My whole body jerks forward and then flops back to the seat as my seatbelt pulls tight across my chest.

"Holy crap, dude," says Quinn. I look back. His eyes are wide. "We almost took out that semi."

"I know. What a rush! That was some nasty driving, Cisco!" I say.

As Cisco hammers his foot on the gas, the tires skid and we shoot across 176th Street. As we fly down 16th Avenue, all I see are farmhouses and open fields on both sides of the car. The limit on this road is 60, but in no time we're doing 120.

"This car moves!" says Quinn.

"That's why you get old cop cars. They have the best engines," says Cisco. "They're sturdy as hell, and move fast! Besides, people see them and get out of your way. They think it's a ghost car."

Quinn and I laugh. We're on our third beer. It's the second week of Spring Break. For the first time, I'm out on the road with both my oldest friend and my buddy Cisco.

As we approach 192nd Street, Cisco leans toward me. "Wanna turn at the wheel?"

Quinn shakes his head as I look at him for support. "Dude, if you lose your licence before you even get it . . ." his voice trails off.

Cisco stops the car by an old cemetery. We hop out and switch places. As I sit in the driver's seat, adrenaline kicks in and I pound the gas pedal. We take off from the side of the road, gravel spewing out behind us. I whip the wheel hard, like Cisco. We skid around the corner onto 192nd Street.

The area is full of new industrial buildings. Half of them aren't even occupied and all of them are closed at night. There are paved roads and gravel roads connecting the buildings. I turn onto a new dirt road. The stench of old garbage assaults our noses and we roll up the windows. Why would you build a business on what used to be the garbage dump?

The beer has made me fearless. I turn the wheel so hard, the car slides along the loose dirt. I have to work to keep us from flying into the fence. My hands grip the wheel and I fight to straighten us out. Then we race down the road. We're lost in a cloud of dust when I finally bring the car to a stop.

I laugh, but I feel sweat dripping down my back. My heart is jumping triple beats in my chest. The guys pile out of the car and high-five me. Cisco pats me on the back then puts his hand out for the keys. That second of panic, when I thought I'd lost control, turns back into excitement at the thrill of the ride.

"Wow," says Cisco. "You handled that turn. I'm impressed!"

"I'm just happy we didn't slam into the fence. Wouldn't want to scratch up the paint job," I reply.

"You'll kick some ass when we street race," Cisco's buddy adds.

"So how does that work?" asks Quinn. His brow tightens as he nods toward the main road.

"We meet here, after midnight. When

it looks like it's all clear, both cars head out to the stop sign for 192nd Street. We rev the engines and wait until it seems like the other guy is ready to go. Then we fly through the intersection along 32nd Avenue. We have, what, about a block and a half of two lanes on our side. Then at the top of the hill, you lose two lanes. You want to be sure you get the lane on the right before you go down the hill. That way you aren't in the one heading into oncoming traffic."

Quinn's eyes widen and he shakes his head. But I'm all over this. "When?" I ask. "When is the next ride? I'm in!"

Before Cisco can answer, Quinn shouts, "Shit, back to the car! Kill the lights!" He points to 32nd Avenue. We see an RCMP vehicle tooling down the road.

We turn off the music and sit in the dark, waiting. My heart booms in my ears. It's beating faster than when I was driving. But the police car passes by. Guess they didn't see us.

Cisco starts the car and heads down 32nd Ave. at regular speed. I think about street racing as we head home. Cisco said one of the dudes he's raced has a blue Mazda GTX turbo. I think I've seen the car around town. What would it be like to race a car like that? I can't wait to drive again.

As we turn into the apartment block, Cisco hands me a six-pack. "I owe you, dude," I say.

"Nah, that one is for the ride!"

My mom is working the late shift, so Quinn and I order a large pizza and head down to the rec room in the basement of the apartment complex. I turn my back to Quinn so he doesn't see me jimmy the lock on the door.

As we dig balls out of the pockets of the pool table, Quinn says, "Dude, tonight was cool. But sometimes I wonder if you have a death wish?"

"What do you mean?"

"Well," he continues. "Think about it. If you get caught street racing, I can't bail you out. I can't fix it if you get screwed for driving illegally."

I break the balls and a striped one drops into a corner pocket. As I line up my next shot I say, "You worry too much, it's all good." I sink another striped ball, but the white cue ball slides into the side pocket.

"Well, I'm glad we didn't meet up with those other guys Cisco races with." Quinn's hand curls around the cue ball. He sets up his shot. Then he knocks a solid into the corner pocket. "The top of the hill is a total blind spot. Then there are just two lanes. What the hell?"

"Yeah," I grin. "One for us and one for them!"

Quinn lines up his cue and smashes the white ball into another solid. As it careens into the pocket, he says, "Not funny. You know that if we have to take the left lane, we go flying over the hill. BAM! Right into a car gunning straight for us. Logan, I don't know about you, but I want to live to see twenty!"

Chapter 4

Three Month Anniversary

"Whoa, take it easy! You won't get your licence this way," says the guy in the passenger seat of the car. I can see him pressing his foot onto the brake he shares with me. The guy really needs to chill. I have plenty of time to stop. He white-knuckles his steering wheel for the last ten minutes of Driver's Ed as we tool around my part of the city. It's June, and the flower beds along the street are in full bloom. At one point, we pass Kayleigh's place. Looks like no one's home. I'll have to catch up with her when I'm done.

As I crawl along 16th Avenue through a playground zone, all I can think about is when I can drive on my own. I can't wait to go street racing, or to fly down Highway 99 to Vancouver. Quinn says taking 99 up to Whistler is even better. Then you have to navigate the curves. Good practice for when I race the SCORE Baja 1000 in Ensenada and destroy the rest of the contestants. Oh, right. The race in Mexico was something Uncle Gerry and I planned to do. Like that will be happening now.

We cruise to a stop just past my school so the next group of kids can get in for their Driver's Ed. A guy from my class is standing on the sidewalk looking nervous.

"How did it go, Gomez?" he asks me as I hop out of the car.

"Other than giving the instructor a heart attack, pretty good."

I jog the six blocks back to Kayleigh's house. I don't knock on the front door in case her dad's home. I don't want to risk another face-to-face like the one on our first date. I steal around to the back side of the house and toss a couple of pebbles at Kayleigh's window. No answer. I pull out my cell phone and my fingers punch out her number. As I wait for her reply, I saunter back to the front street.

"Hey, Logan," she says into the phone. Her voice is raspy. She sounds like Janis Joplin on the old vinyl Uncle Gerry used to listen to. "What's up?"

It's our three-month anniversary and I love how she's acting all cool. Like it's not a special day. I have a present to surprise her. "Well," I say. "I was thinking I could take you out for fish and chips. How about we meet at seven o'clock?"

Kayleigh is being hassled by her parents to do well so she'll get a scholarship to UBC. I'm glad I don't have that kind of stress from my mom. Kayleigh was pissed that she had to study over lunch hour and that we couldn't see each other at school.

She says yes to my suggestion of dinner. We decide to meet down at the White Rock Pier. That way, when we finish eating, we can walk along the beach and I can give her the gift I picked out.

It usually takes me a good twenty minutes from Kayleigh's house to the apartment, but today I make it in record time. I grab the mail from our box, and feel a pang of guilt as I sift through nothing but bills. I'm supposed to be helping Mom out with costs. My cell phone, clothes for school, extra groceries — that sort of thing. And here I am taking Kayleigh out for dinner, which will be another $30 on top of the $30 I spent on her gift.

I seem to burn through the bucks I earn at Zellers, stocking shelves. Even our monthly donation from Uncle Gerry doesn't last long, although I wish we could do without his guilt money. But there are only two weeks left of school, and I'll take on extra shifts for the summer to make more cash. It will all balance out. I brush away the bad feelings and hop in the shower.

At the pier, Kayleigh is waiting for me. She looks just as hot as the day I met her. She is wearing a black and white striped skirt and sandals. Her blue tank top matches her eyes and her long black hair is pulled behind her ears. She takes me in her arms for a kiss. Her lips are smooth and I can taste her raspberry lip gloss.

I had planned to give her the gift after dinner, but I'm too excited to wait so I plop the package into her hand.

"What's this?" she asks.

"Ah, it's ah . . . a gift. You know, for our anniversary. Three months!" I hope I look calm, but my hands are shaking.

She opens the wrapping to reveal dream-catcher earrings. I bought them at Cheryl's Trading Post in the Semiahmoo Mall. I discovered on one of our dates that Kayleigh loves First Nations art. So she's squealing with excitement as she puts them in her ears. I like how the left one dangles by her peace symbol tattoo, showing it off. She kisses me again.

"These are amazing, Logan. And you're taking me for dinner too. Are you sure about this?"

"Absolutely," I say. "No problem."

After we eat, we chill and watch the sunset. Then we walk along the beach, lit only by the moonlight. Kayleigh threads her fingers through mine.

Further down the beach we pass four guys I recognize as seniors from our school. One of them kicks sand at me as we get close.

"What the hell?" I say, bristling, ready for a fight.

Kayleigh squeezes my hand. It's her way of saying, 'don't mess with them'. I let it go, but the jerk gets inside my head. I could use a beer to calm the tension rolling through my shoulders. Just past the metal stairs and bridge that go over the train track, I get my wish.

It's Cisco and his buddies, hanging around a fire they lit with some driftwood.

"Amigo, how's it going?" Cisco puts his fist out to meet mine. He grins as he looks Kayleigh over. Then he puts his arm around my shoulder, and nods at one of his buddies. The guy passes me a beer. "So, when are we cruising again?"

"Just name the time and I'm there!" I down the beer fast and Cisco sends another one my way. Kayleigh is slow dancing to some tunes playing from a guy's cell phone. Her eyes sparkle in the fire's glow. I slide close to her and she shares my beer. After a few sips, I lock lips with her. The guys whistle. It's the perfect way to end the day.

It's late when I walk Kayleigh home. We sneak around to the back of the house.

"Thanks for a great three-month anniversary. And for my gift." She twirls a dream-catcher earring with one hand, and slides her other arm around my waist. "One more kiss and then I have to go. If my folks find out you and I were together, they'll kill me."

We linger in each other's arms for a few minutes. Then I watch her head into the house. I walk back to the street and grin all the way home.

Chapter 5

Tested

It's the last week of school. I just finished my Workplace Math exam and am heading out the door to the smoke pit. After that brutal test, I need a cigarette. One of the guys hanging there offers me a butt. I have a few puffs and then my cell buzzes. It's a text from Kayleigh. All it says is, "OMG!"

My fingers punch back, "What's up?"

Kayleigh's response is quick. "Dad totally on my ass. Can we meet? On my way to the park."

"See you in 10."

I meet Kayleigh in the park by my apartment. She kisses me, then slides her hand into mine. Geese are sprawled on the grass, their goslings wobbling around them. The park is a total seniors' hang out. A guy passing us on his scooter almost clips us. I am about to yell at him when Kayleigh puts her arm over mine.

"You don't have to be in class right now, do you?"

"Nope," I answer back.

"Can we hang at your place for a while?"

"Won't your dad flip if he finds out you're skipping class?" I ask.

She smiles. "Since when did you become the champion of *doing the right thing*?"

"Since I . . ." I hesitate. The right words don't come. "Since I decided to run interference between you and your dad."

"Well, I need to decompress or I'm going to explode. My dad is stressing because I got a C on my Humanities paper. Now he assumes

I've flunked the test. Somehow, he thinks this is your fault."

Great! I haven't done anything and I'm to blame. I feel my body heat up and my heart pumps faster.

"Ow!" says Kayleigh. "Not so tight. You're squeezing my hand."

"Sorry. It's just, your dad doesn't know me, and he doesn't want to get to know me. How fair is that? Does he still think I'm in a gang? Why do you let him . . ."

"I DON'T let him. He has this crazy idea I should be going with a guy on his way to being our next prime minister. He has no idea who I am. He has no idea what I like, or who I like." A tear half escapes her eye and she quickly rubs it away. "Can we just go to your place and chill?"

"Sure. I didn't mean to give you a hard time. Look, I'll even help you study."

We both laugh.

"See how fast you can make me relax?" she says, as we near the garage entrance to my building. She leans in and kisses my cheek. Before we head up to my apartment, I stop at the storage room and grab the last of the beer that Cisco bought me.

"What's that for? Don't you have your English test this afternoon?" she asks.

"Yeah, but you said you wanted to chill."

As we enter my apartment, she kicks off her shoes and heads for the couch. As she sprawls across it, I crack open the beer and pour it into a glass.

"I really don't want one, Logan. I still have my Pre-Calc exam and need to have a clear head."

I shrug my shoulders and press the cool glass to my lips. I offer Kayleigh a juice. Then I fall onto the couch beside her.

"My dad doesn't get it," says Kayleigh. "You are so lucky that your mom lets you do your own thing. With my dad working from home half the time, I can't even relax there. I'm sure he has spies at the school."

"I've watched you these past months. You put in an effort. Your dad should cut you some slack."

"I know, right? And there's something else I haven't told you. Know how we have to complete volunteer work in order to graduate? Dad thinks I'm behind already. So today he tells me he's picked a spot for me to do my time. Can you believe it? He knows a person on the board at some community centre. I start tomorrow."

"That sucks," I say. "Are you going to have to do this for the whole summer?"

"I think it's something like five hours a week."

"That's a lot!" I do the math. Between my job and Kayleigh's volunteer hours, it doesn't leave us much time together. "Is it because of me?" My temples pulse.

"What do you mean?"

"This might be your dad's way of making sure we don't see each other."

She leans her head against my shoulder. "You could be right. But trust me, I'm not going to let my dad stand in the way of us being together."

I run my fingers through her hair.

Kayleigh continues, "You know, when we first met I liked you for two reasons. One, you're super hot and my girlfriends are totally jealous. And two, I knew it would piss my dad off." She looks up at me and grins. "But you know, you're actually a pretty good listener."

"Only *pretty good*?" I tickle her and she laughs, rolling back onto the couch. I move in to kiss her lips, my body hovering over hers.

"Wait," she stops me. "Are you sure your mom won't come home?"

"No, she's on day shifts. Next week, she'll be on nights." I move close to her mouth again. "Is this okay?" I ask. She meets my lips.

We're still tangled in each other's arms when her alarm goes off, telling us it's time to head back to class.

We find Hayden and Quinn hanging by his locker. Hayden and Kayleigh hit it off as soon as they met, and now they're BFFs. They put their arms around each other and wave goodbye as they head down the hall.

Quinn leans in to talk to me. "Dude, you totally missed second block. Where were you? I can smell booze on your breath. Are you serious? What the hell?"

I pop gum in my mouth and turn away from Quinn.

He puts his arm on my shoulder. "Come on, man. I'm just looking out for you. Let's wait and grab a beer after school. You shouldn't do that shit in the daytime."

Someone taps my shoulder. I turn around, trying not to freak out when I see it's Mr. Williamson. "What did you just say?" he asks Quinn.

"Ah, nothing, Mr. Williamson. Logan and I are going to be late for class. Gotta run!"

***

Two days into summer break, Hayden, Quinn, Kayleigh and I pick up our report cards and then head out for lunch. Kayleigh and I spend all afternoon at the park. It's supper time when I head back to my apartment to get ready for my shift at Zellers. I pour myself a glass of OJ and wolf down a grilled cheese sandwich in a few bites. Then I head to work. It's only across the street to the mall, so I have enough time to finish a cigarette on the way.

Zellers is at the far end of the mall. My boss looks shocked when he sees me, like he doesn't remember he booked me for today.

I have a four-hour shift, so I start in the storage room. The week's deliveries are all there and the place is one big mess of boxes. But I like the work. I don't get to run the equipment, but lifting heavy boxes gives me a pretty good workout. Tonight, I'm working with this twenty-something-year-old who started three

56

days ago. So far, all he has done is bad-mouth me.

"Hey, *fruit picker* — pass me a bottle of water, will ya."

"So, what did you do yesterday?" I ask him. "Surf the net for racial slurs?" I hurl the water bottle at him. He catches it just before it whacks him in the head.

"Watch it, asshole! I'm in good with the boss. You don't want to mess with me. I could get you fired from this job. Or maybe deported back to whatever third-world country you come from."

I roll my eyes and get back to work. As long as I do my job, I am pretty sure I won't get fired. But with this new jerk, I'll have to keep my temper in check. That might be hard, since he seems to enjoy pushing my buttons.

As the evening wears on, I feel my chest tighten and I seem to be using a lot of energy lifting boxes I could usually handle quite easily. Then it hits me: my body is preparing for the stress of tomorrow — my dad's birthday.

Once I get home, I realize I'm out of vodka and brew. Mom only has wine in the cupboard. I know one bottle is a gift from last Christmas she never opened. She won't know it's missing.

Chapter 6

Invincible

The phone rings. It's the third time today. There is no way in hell I am answering it.

Mom hollers from the kitchen, "Will you get that, Logan? It's your Uncle Geraldo."

Like I don't already know who it is. And he won't stop calling. Not until this day is over.

Today would have been my dad's fortieth birthday.

I look at the photo on my desk. It was taken when my mom and dad first got together. In the picture, one of my dad's arms is around my mom's waist. The other arm is straight out from his side. Three steelhead trout dangle from a wire stringer. Mom says I have his smile. He sure was grinning that day.

Fishing was something my dad loved, but boating was always a family event. Taking the boat out on the lake for their birthdays was my dad and Uncle Gerry's 'thing'. Uncle Gerry used to say they had planned to celebrate that way until they were in their nineties. But he ruined that plan.

Forever.

The phone stops ringing. I lie down on my bed and grab my pillow. I hug it close to my chest and try to regulate my breathing. I hear my mom's heels clacking on the hardwood floor, which means she's on her way to my room. I jump out of bed and slam the door shut. Just as it closes I spot her face in the hallway. Her face is flushed and there are tears in her eyes.

Great! Now I feel like an asshole. *Thanks, Uncle Gerry!*

I flop back down on my bed and put my earbuds in. Before I can push play on my antique MP3 player, Mom's voice comes through the door.

"Logan, you can't ignore him forever. Please, be reasonable."

I crank my tunes so I can't hear her next comment. I know my mom's routine. She'll shuffle down the hall and lock herself in her bedroom for the next few hours. Mom and I do this day solo now.

I've taken Uncle Gerry's pictures off the wall, but I can't forget all the Sundays we spent together. We'd go boating or hang at the park and shoot baskets. He'd take me to an afternoon movie or out for ice cream. Those *were* the best days ever.

But that was before I knew the truth.

My throat constricts. It feels like I swallowed a jawbreaker. As much as I hate thinking about the past, today, it feels like I have no control.

I curl my hand into a fist and bang my bedroom wall. Since the paint is chipped in that spot, a few flecks fall onto my blanket.

I can't stop the flood of memories, or the anger. Both come. Like they always do.

I know what my uncle wants, but I'm not going to give it to him.

I can't stay in the house another minute. As I pass Mom's room on my way to the front door, I can hear her sobbing. This is all on my uncle. Why did he have to screw things up?

I want to drive to Quinn's place, but my learner's permit means I have to have an adult in the car. So I grab my bike out of the parking garage and jump on. I haven't ridden it much lately and I feel a burn in my quads as I pedal down the street.

The faster I go, the quicker the thoughts fly out of my head. Adrenaline pumps through me. All I can see is the grey of the road and the flash of sun reflected off the parked cars I pass. Faster and faster my legs push. And the wheels respond.

As my bike flies toward Oxford Street, I rest my legs and coast. Like I am ten again, I throw my arms up in the air and keep my balance just with my knees. The warm summer air feels cool as it passes along my bare arms. Once I reach Oxford Street, my bike will scream down the steep hill. It will be murder to keep my balance.

Ahead, the light on 16th Avenue turns yellow as I approach. I pedal harder. I bite my lip as I push my head down into the wind I've created with my own speed. My heart pumps into overdrive. I glance up just as the light turns red. My bike flies into the intersection.

A horn blasts.

I barely turn my head. But it is enough to make me lose my balance.

The front tire slides out from beneath me and twists the handlebars. I hear the screech

of car tires and brakes jamming. My bike falls
to the ground, my leg caught between it and
the road. It keeps sliding on its side along the
pavement. Gravel and asphalt rip my skin and
a burn flashes through my brain.

When I finally skid to a stop someone is
already bending over me.

"Jesus, are you all right, kid?" a man's voice
says. I blink up into the sunlight. A blur of
white hair is all I can make out. A gnarled hand
reaches for my shoulder and helps me to sit up.
I'm finding it hard to breathe.

Another person bends down. It's the driver
of the car.

"Oh my god — the light turned green. I
just drove through. I didn't see you coming.
Can you move your leg?" The woman gasps, as
she looks at the stream of red visible through
my ripped jeans. I can taste blood in my
mouth.

The woman opens her cell phone. "I'll
call for an ambulance. Oh my god, what have

I done?" She paces back and forth, her body shaking.

"It's okay, ma'am," says the white-haired guy. "The boy will be fine. He's just a bit shaken up." He stands up and puts his hand on the woman's trembling shoulder. "*He* ran the red light. You couldn't have done anything."

I holler at him, "I didn't *run* the red light. I just . . . I wanted to . . ." I can't remember why I felt compelled to race. It's as though I became invincible the moment the light changed. And as I move my leg and realize the old guy is right — that I am okay — I feel the adrenaline rush through me again.

I stand up. My legs threaten to buckle under me, but I hold my balance. My bike lies in the middle of the road, trashed. The lady is still holding her cell phone but hasn't dialed any numbers. And suddenly, I begin to laugh — a deep, throaty laugh.

The old guy shakes his head at me.

"Wow! I can't believe I SURVIVED."

I walk a few steps. My flesh is ripped open but obviously I haven't broken anything. Other than a cut on my leg and a crunched arm, I am all right.

I drag my mangled bike to the curb and sit down. Shielding my eyes from the sun, I survey the scene. Several people have gathered on the road and are staring at me. Two tweens have their cell phones pointed in my direction. I give them the finger and they take off down the street.

The old guy leans into the lady's car. It looks like they are exchanging papers. Maybe they are taking each other's phone number, in case I press charges or something? I feel dizzy but figure it's all the excitement. Now I can't wait to get to Quinn's place and tell him what happened. I hope he'll have some food too. I am starving.

Chapter 7

After the Crash

Since it's Saturday, Quinn's mom is home. She fusses over me like I am still seven. She grabs peroxide and cotton balls. As her hand moves toward my leg, I take the supplies from her and smile. "I'm good, Mrs. B."

She looks at the cut down my shin, filled with embedded gravel. "Logan, you should at least let your mom know what happened. In case you have a break or need stitches."

"Don't worry. I'll fill her in when I get

home. Besides, she'll be relieved to see I wasn't hurt."

"You call this not hurt?" says Quinn, staring at the gaping hole below my knee.

Ever since we were kids, I've always been the one who got scraped up, fell out of trees and did faceplants when we played games. Quinn has always picked me up and let me lean on his shoulder to get home.

"I thought you'd gotten used to this by now?" I laugh.

Quinn and his mom shake their heads at the same time. He brings me a Coke and opens a bag of chips.

"Quinn, don't eat those. I'll make you some sandwiches. I bet you're starving, Logan."

"Thanks, Mrs. B." She nailed that one. Adrenaline and excitement are massive fuel burners.

Quinn and I let his mom make us lunch while we head out to his porch with our Cokes and the bag of chips.

"What the hell, dude?" says Quinn. He sits down, stretching out his long legs beyond the steps. His eyes are on the grass, where my bike lies with its bent tires, warped handlebars and dangling pedals.

"I don't know. I saw the yellow light and something pushed me forward. I didn't see or hear any cars, it was just me against the light." As I sit down beside him, pain shoots up my leg. I feel my face contort as I take in short breaths.

"Right," he snorts. "And now that you've had your *daily dose of excitement*, how do you figure we'll top that this afternoon?"

It is the beginning of summer, and we have time to kill. I have two days off before my next shift at Zellers. Even though Quinn has added new streets to his paper route, we're looking at loads of free time over the summer break.

"I dunno," I answer. "Maybe we should call Kayleigh and Hayden? See what they're up to."

Mrs. B steps onto the porch and sits a plate down between us. It is loaded with ham sandwiches, little cheese pieces wrapped in cellophane and grapes and strawberries. I grab a sandwich and start munching.

"I phoned your mom, Logan. She wants you to call home when you finish your lunch."

I sigh. "Thanks for the food."

"You call her, okay?" Her print dress swishes as she returns to the house.

Quinn looks at me sideways. "Sorry, bro."

"Your mom should mind her own business! Come on," I put the half-sandwich back on the plate and pocket five of the little cheeses. When I stand up blood rushes to my head and I feel dizzy. I have to lean on Quinn's shoulder for support.

"Are you okay?" he asks.

"Yeah. *I'm fine.* And I'd be even better if everyone would *leave me the hell alone.*"

He pushes my hand off his shoulder. He looks as though he is about to retreat into his house.

"Dude, I'm sorry," I backtrack quickly. "I don't mean *you*." I get my footing back and turn to face Quinn. "Look, I'm pissed with my stupid family. The phone has been ringing all day. Uncle Gerry and his ritual of guilt."

"Shit, why didn't you say something? I forgot it's the anniversary of your dad's . . ."

I cut him off, "*Birthday*. Yeah. It's that time of year." Thinking about how I lost my dad boils my blood and I feel tense all over again.

I hobble down the steps. Quinn's black Labrador rushes up to the plate and grabs my half-eaten sandwich with his teeth.

"Manny, *no!*" Quinn lunges toward the dog, but Manny is off the porch and around the corner of the house in seconds.

My stomach is still growling for food. Using my good leg, I hop back up the stairs. I grab another sandwich. It disappears in five bites. Taking out my cell, I dial Kayleigh's number while Quinn and I hit the sidewalk at a slow pace. When we round the corner, we head toward Centennial Park.

"Hey, Logan," Kayleigh says into the phone.

"So, Kay, we were wondering if you and Hayden are doing anything right now? Want to come hang with Quinn and me?"

"Sure, where should we meet up?" she asks.

"At the park. We're on our way there now."

As I hang up, Quinn pushes the button to cross the street. Sixteenth Avenue is one of the busiest roads in White Rock. As cars whiz past us I look down at my ripped jeans. My leg is cut up, but it could have been worse. I could have been a mangled mess in the middle of the road.

When we arrive at the park, four little kids are on the equipment. As soon as we step onto the playground, they run.

I open the cellophane packages and pull the string that rips the red wax casing to reveal the cheese. I plop three in my mouth at once, and wish I'd grabbed another sandwich. I'm still starving. Quinn hangs upside down on the monkey bars.

My cell vibrates. I flip the lid and see it is my home number. I don't feel like dealing with my mom at the moment, so I pocket it without answering.

"Was that Kayleigh?" asks Quinn.

"Naw, it was my mom."

"Dude, she's just worried. You know how she gets around this time. And then you go and almost get yourself killed on your bike. When you used to see your uncle, it made the birthdays easier on everyone. You know he was just . . ."

I cut him off. "He was just a murdering asshole! He lied for years. Making me care about him. Making me replace my dad with him. What did he think would happen when I discovered the truth?" Dust spews as I kick the sand by the swings.

"Maybe he thought you'd understand?

Maybe he hoped you'd forgive him?"

"Right," I straddle the bottom of the slide and plop down. As I bend my leg, I feel a burn again. Now I like the pain. It is comforting.

"Why don't we . . ."

"Why don't we just LET IT GO."

Chapter 8

Gingerbread Man

I look in Quinn's direction, but he avoids eye contact. I don't understand why he can't see things my way — why he can't see how I feel cheated. He should know better than anyone what I lost. Just then Kayleigh and Hayden arrive.

"Hey, guys," says Hayden. She runs up and kisses Quinn on the cheek. He grins and flips off the bars, then pulls her close and hugs her. He runs his fingers through her blue and white streaked hair. The three of us have been friends since we were four. But for the last year, Hayden and Quinn have been dating.

Kayleigh leans down to give me a hug as soon as she reaches me. I half lose my balance and suck in air. My injured leg burns when I dig my heels into the ground. She holds me at arm's length and looks at my torn pants.

"What the hell? What did you do?" she makes a face. "Are you okay?"

"He was pretending to be Superman," snickers Quinn.

"I just got clipped at the light, that's all."

"You got hit by a car?" asks Hayden. I can see Quinn shaking his head at my half-lie. He doesn't say anything.

"Well, sort of. I mean, not really. I wiped out on my bike because I almost got clipped," I shoot a glare at Quinn.

"Jeez. I'm glad you're all right," Kayleigh kisses me. She smells like cinnamon and sugar and I can taste the buttery mixture on her lips.

I hope I don't stink like bad cheese. As we pull apart I grab a stick of gum from my pocket and pop it into my mouth.

"So, what's the plan?" asks Hayden, still in Quinn's arms.

"Let's snag some booze from Kelly's Off Sales and find a hangout," I reply. The buzz from the accident is wearing off. I need something else to make my memory of today a blur.

"Right, and how do you figure we'll get beer?" asks Quinn.

"No problem — Cisco!"

Cisco is waiting with our beer when we arrive at the liquor store. I hand him thirty bucks. That's the last of my cash until payday except for a couple of toonies that jingle in my pocket.

"So, where should we go?" asks Quinn as Cisco squeals out of the parking lot.

"My place is definitely out," answers Kayleigh. "We've got family in from Winnipeg. How about your place, Logan? I've got my swimsuit in my bag."

It's great weather and our complex has an outdoor pool.

As I stall for an answer, Quinn jumps in. "His mom's home. Not a good day for Logan's place. Next idea?"

"Listen, I've got a plan," I say. "How about we check out Old Ginger's place? If he's out of town, no one will see or hear us." There is a long driveway to the old guy's house back among the trees.

"Old Ginger," says Kayleigh. "You mean the guy has red hair?"

Quinn laughs. "No, the nickname is short for Gingerbread Man. Remember, Logan, how your uncle . . ."

I cut him short with a glare. It was Uncle Gerry who first corrected our mistake when we were young. I look at the ground, trying to keep my emotions in check. We are almost in the park again. My breath comes in short bursts as I think about Uncle Gerry.

"We called him that when we were kids because he lived on Dreary Lane," says Hayden.

"That's right," Quinn pipes in. "We thought the nursery rhyme said 'Dreary Lane' was where the Gingerbread Man lived. Turns out it was not only the wrong name for the street, but the wrong nursery rhyme."

"That's enough, Quinn!" I blurt out the words, my voice tight. I don't need memories of my uncle surfacing again. Quinn bows his head.

Kayleigh moves beside me. She takes my right arm and places it around her waist. I love the feel of her skin as my fingers slip into the familiar space between the top of her shorts and her tank top.

Hayden continues, "Yeah, the nursery rhyme was about the *Muffin Man* who lived on *Drury Lane*."

To steer us away from more talk that leads to memories of Uncle Gerry, I say, "It doesn't matter why we called the guy Gingerbread Man. Let's just find out if Old Ginger is home or not. I want to party!"

Kayleigh pulls me closer as we cross the street. We haven't agreed to go there, but I find myself steering us toward Dreary Lane.

Quinn joins hands with Hayden as we cross the street. Then Hayden pipes up, "Old Ginger is strange. We hardly see him around town. I don't know what his story is, but I hear he's quite a loner."

"That's kind of sad," says Kayleigh.

"I know he has been out of town lots of times," says Quinn. "Like right now. I've jammed his papers in the mailbox, but it's full. So now I'm chucking them down his driveway, hoping to get them in his carport. I'm not sure how long he's been away, but I bet there are twenty or thirty papers in his yard."

We are at the forested area that lines that

end of Dreary Lane. I lean against a tree and take out a cigarette and light it.

"I thought you quit," says Kayleigh, looking irritated.

"Sort of. It didn't bother you that much before."

She puts her hand in mine. "I know. I guess . . . things are changing?" Kayleigh's right. I think about how my feelings for her get stronger the more I get to know her. And it's like she really cares about what happens to me now. I drop the cigarette on the forest floor and stomp on it. A thin line of smoke rises up from the ground, so Kayleigh pushes her sandal into it again.

"Well . . ." I say. "What's our plan?"

"I think we should scope the place out. See if Old Ginger is home. If he isn't, maybe we can hang in his yard," says Quinn. "It would be fun if we could party somewhere away from the street."

"I agree," adds Hayden. "But maybe

you guys should see if he's around. If it looks deserted, then we can come back tonight, when it's dark?"

Now that we are focused on partying, I can almost taste the cool beer sliding down my throat. Getting a little drunk will definitely get rid of any thoughts of my uncle. "Right," I say out loud. "We'll meet here later with a plan, some drinks and loads of attitude!" I lift Kayleigh off the ground and twirl her around. She smiles and bends her head down to kiss me.

"I'm in," smiles Kayleigh.

"Ditto," says Quinn.

Chapter 9

Busted

Quinn says he wants to chill before we party with the girls. We agree to meet at Old Ginger's place early so we can check things out and get a head start on the beer.

I'm thinking that we might as well make the most of Old Ginger being away. Why not break into the place and party inside? Who knows, maybe he'll even have some things I can steal to help out with my cash flow problem.

Quinn heads home, and I walk to the gas

station on Johnston and Thrift. I'm hungry, but the four bucks in my pocket won't go very far. I pick up a chocolate bar and then put it back on the shelf. I fill the biggest cup with a frozen cola drink and look around. There's only one dude working in the small store and he's gone out to pump gas for an old lady. There's a guy in the repair bay with his head under the hood of a car, inspecting the engine. I reach for the chocolate bar again. I'm just about to pocket it, without paying, when the store phone rings.

It surprises me and I lose my grip on the iced drink. It slides from my hands and splashes onto the floor and my pants. The guy in the service garage looks up and yells, "Shit!" His eyes burn into mine. I slap my toonies and the chocolate bar onto the counter and fly out of the gas station, empty-handed. I bolt past the dude pumping gas.

Once on the street, my feet carry me toward home. Since I let Quinn take the beer to his place, I have nothing to help me release the stress. I could definitely use a drink to calm my nerves now. Maybe I'll have to check out more of Mom's stuff?

I enter our apartment quietly, hoping Mom's gone out. But I find her sitting at the table with half-empty bottles of liquor and wine spread out in front of her.

"Thirsty, Mom?" I ask.

"This is no joke, Logan. First, it's suspensions at school. Now, this?"

"What do you mean?" I ask, feeling my fingers knot into fists.

"You know what I mean. You're sixteen. A glass of wine with supper is no big deal. But sneaking drinks behind my back? What's going on, Logan?"

"I meant to replace the wine, Mom. I just forgot." I think fast. "It's just . . . it was . . . our date night. Kayleigh and I had some wine while I made dinner. We didn't even finish it. I meant to tell you." I take a deep breath.

"Now you are insulting me by lying. I

didn't want to confront you, because I know today is hard for you. But it seems to be getting worse every year, instead of better. With that suspension for fighting and your skipping school to do God-knows-what with Cisco all the time, I worry about you. I think we need some help."

Like her words are a signal, the door buzzer from downstairs sounds. I didn't know Mom was expecting anyone. She talks into the phone for the front entrance and says, "Glad you're here." Then she pushes the button to release the main door. She flings the apartment door wide and waits. A moment later she peers out into the hall.

"Geraldo," she says. "Thanks for coming on such short notice."

"What!" I yell.

Uncle Gerry gives me a half-smile as he steps into our doorway. The first thing I think is how much he has aged in four years. He looks ancient. He puts his hand out, like he wants to shake mine.

I knock past him and fly down the hall.

I barely register Uncle Gerry's face as I run past. But the look of shock, the hurt look in his eyes follows me. I hear him calling *Mi hijo* as I run down the hall to the stairs.

I don't slow down until I find myself at Old Ginger's place.

I bang my fist against the trunk of a tree in his backyard. The bark scratches my flesh and blood drips onto the grass. I rub my hand and try to steady my breathing.

I could use a drink. Maybe it would help fill the hole I feel in my gut from seeing Uncle Gerry after all this time. It doesn't help that he looks ruined by the years. He seems ragged and broken. Is that because of what he did? Or is it because I know the truth?

For four years I've been able to keep Uncle Gerry out of my life because I've only had to deal with phone calls. Seeing him threw me off guard. I'm glad I'm in Old Ginger's yard before the others. I need time to clear my head so I'm 'on' for the party.

I climb up the tree and perch on a branch. I am able to see past the house to the other homes in the area. They are a good distance away, which means probably no one will hear us tonight. I can concentrate on partying and getting cozy with Kayleigh. Anything to get the look on Uncle Gerry's face out of my mind.

Even after an hour, there is no activity from within the house. No movement. Nada. It's pretty clear Old Ginger is out of town.

Chapter 10

Breaking . . .

I must have dozed off because I hear a SNAP and nearly fall out of the tree.

"*Dude*," Quinn whispers. "What are you doing up there?"

I jump down to stand beside him. As I land, I feel pain fly up my hurt leg. I hop on the good one until the pulsing ache is gone. "I needed a spot . . . for surveillance," I say between short breaths. Then I realize my bladder is about to explode. I turn my back to

Quinn and unzip my pants. As I pee into the bushes I hear him rustle through his pack.

"What'd you bring?" I ask, turning back to face him. The moon is half-hidden by the clouds but the sky is still bright.

"A flashlight." He pulls it out and turns it on, flashing it up toward the sky.

"Don't shine it in the windows!" I push his hand down so the light hits the ground. A few old leaves roll across the path.

"What — is he home? Did you see him?"

"No," I answer as I walk closer to the house. "But you never know."

Quinn laughs. "I think you've been out here too long. Have some food." He rummages in his pack again and pulls out a bag of cheezies and a bag of chips. "Which one do you want?"

"Are you kidding? Both, of course." I pull the bag of cheezies out of his hand and rip it open. After three handfuls I'm thirsty. "Did you remember the beer?"

"'Course! And I snuck a bottle of vodka from the liquor cabinet. Well, actually, it was a bottle of Kirsch. But there were only a few drops left so I emptied it out in the sink and poured vodka from my brother's magnum into the bottle. Do you think he'll miss it?"

"Mr. 'I want to be an accountant'? I think so!"

He kicks at some loose twigs. "Guess I should have added water to his vodka so he wouldn't notice." He reaches into his knapsack and pulls out the bottle and his favourite cap. I know the cap is his favourite, because it is the one he got on his last trip to San Francisco. His family even invited me to join them, but there was no way Mom could afford to send me. Quinn passes me the bottle and places his cap on his head.

I take a swig of the vodka. It tastes like cough medicine, so I spit it out. "Shit! I thought you said you washed the bottle?"

"I didn't say that. I just dumped what was

in there and added the new stuff. I was in a hurry and didn't want to get caught." He grabs the bottle from my hand and takes a drink. "It's not that bad."

I get hold of Quinn's knapsack and take out a six-pack of beer. I open a can and swig most of it.

"So, I have an idea," I say. "The place is dark. The papers are all over. It's pretty clear the guy's out of town. I say we party *inside*."

"But what if the neighbours hear us and call the police?"

"We were already planning to party in his yard. We keep the lights off and the music low. It's all good." The idea of breaking in gives me a bit of a rush.

Quinn's mind must be on a similar track, because he says, "Okay, but let's get in *before* the girls arrive. Then we can say the door was unlocked."

"Do you think that makes a difference?" I ask.

"Yeah. If he leaves his door open it's like an invitation. If it's locked, well, we're . . ." He doesn't finish the sentence.

"Check this out," I say. I move toward the back porch, grabbing the flashlight as I pass him. I shine it around the door. "Maybe he has a key hidden here. You know, for when he locks himself out?"

"Brilliant," says Quinn, cracking open a beer for himself and another one for me. I'd hoped Cisco would get us a two-four. But there are only eighteen cans. Hayden and Kayleigh won't want very much, especially if they like that vile concoction that Quinn has. But it occurs to me that maybe we should space the beers out a bit.

Quinn checks around the door frame and I move my hand over the ledge by the sliding door. We both come up empty. I lift the mat in front of the door, but all it reveals is a square, clean patch on the cement and a spider. It seems pissed at me for disturbing its home.

To the right of the door is what looks like a cupboard. "What's this for?" I ask. "Is it like a cat door or something?"

Quinn smiles. "My grandpa's house had one. It's an old milk chute for when they used to deliver milk door to door."

The thought of milk sitting in that cupboard during a hot summer day, curdling into chunky lumps, makes the beer in my stomach churn. I curl my fingers around the small knob and pull. It doesn't open. Quinn and I take turns trying to pry open the door, but it is stuck.

I pull my jack-knife from my pocket. As soon as I slide it around the edges of the door, the milk chute snaps open. Unfortunately, there's no key sitting on the ledge. My shoulders slump and I plop down on the porch.

Quinn pushes past me and sticks his hand into the opening of the milk chute. He turns his hand around the insides, feeling every square inch. "Sweet!" he exclaims. He pulls out a dull silver key. "It was taped to the top of the chute."

We can get into the house! We give each other a high-five.

The moon has settled behind the trees. We are almost in total darkness. A summer breeze breaks the stillness of the air. As it pushes the branches into one another, they crackle. The wind picks up and blows a flyer across the grass in front of us. At the sight of that white form floating across the yard, I feel a cold prickle lift the hairs on my neck.

I hold the flashlight so it lights up the door. Quinn and I look at each other. Quinn shrugs his shoulders. I take it to mean that I should open the door. I push the key into the handle and turn it. The door unlocks. Before I can push it open, something comes running at us from the bushes. I pull the key out of the lock as we turn to see what it is.

Chapter 11

. . . And Entering

"Gotcha!" laughs Kayleigh as she runs up the porch stairs to my side. Hayden hugs Quinn but he pushes her away.

"What gives?" he asks.

"Aw, come on . . . we didn't scare you, did we?" Hayden laughs. Quinn shrugs, then grabs her by the waist and tickles her. Kayleigh and I lock lips as I slide the key into the pocket of my jeans.

When we pull apart, I ask, "Who's up for a

drink?" All three answer 'me' at the same time. While the girls sip their beers, Quinn and I take huge gulps.

"I also brought some cherry-flavoured vodka," smiles Quinn.

Both Kayleigh and Hayden take swigs from the bottle he offers.

"Wow — this is good," says Hayden.

Quinn smirks in my direction.

I pull out my cigarettes and Kayleigh gives me a disgusted look. "I'm just going to have two puffs." I light the cigarette, inhale twice then squeeze the end to put it out. I place the cigarette behind my ear for later. I am beginning to feel a buzz.

Kayleigh takes a handful of chips from the open bag. She feeds me some while she nibbles. Hayden pulls her phone from her backpack and sits it on the edge of the porch with her mini-speakers.

"We should turn that way down," I say. "The old guy is definitely out of town, but we don't want the neighbours to hear."

"The houses are pretty far apart. I'm sure we're okay," says Hayden.

"But it seems *too* quiet out here," says Kayleigh, shuddering as she speaks. "Kind of eerie. It wouldn't take much noise to stand out."

What Kayleigh says reminds me of how sound used to travel across Harrison Lake when I went boating with Uncle Gerry. I shake my head and swallow more beer to chase away the memory.

Hayden turns the volume down so low we have to form a tight group to hear it. I don't mind. It means the girls stay close to us. Kayleigh and I sway back and forth in a slow dance. Hayden and Quinn hold hands and whisper to each other.

"I'm glad Gingerbread Man is on holidays," says Hayden after we've listened to several tunes.

I reply, "I know, right?" This is it. I take a breath before speaking. "You know, we also found out the back door's unlocked."

"Really?" asks Hayden.

"Yeah . . . kind of like an invitation to go in," adds Quinn, looking at me sideways.

"I don't know," says Kayleigh. "Do you think it's safe?"

"Safe . . . yeah," answers Hayden. "But I don't know if it's a good idea. I mean it will be just as much fun partying out here. If we go inside, we're breaking and entering."

"Only *entering*," I correct her.

"Still . . ." she pauses and looks at Quinn.

"It doesn't really matter if we party out here or in there," he says. "It's pretty much the same. Either way, we have to remember not to turn on any lights, and to keep the volume and our voices down."

As if what Quinn is saying is a signal, the wind blows in some low clouds. They shroud the sliver of moon visible between the trees, making it completely dark. And they release faint drops of rain.

"Gotta love living on the west coast," laughs Quinn. "We can stay out here and get wet, or we can go inside. You guys decide."

Hayden and Kayleigh trade glances. Then Kayleigh looks at me. I shrug my shoulders. "Sometimes, you've gotta live dangerously!"

"Okay, *fine*," says Hayden.

We each open a new beer and grab the supplies as we move toward the back door. Even though I am certain that we won't get caught, the thought that we are breaking the law sharpens my mind through the beer buzz. My nerves spark with a cooling sensation that travels down my arms and legs. My heart kicks up its rhythm and my pulse quickens.

The silence is eerie, just like Kayleigh said. I look at my three friends. Their faces have lost some of their colour, and the darkness makes their eyes solid black.

The door creaks as I push it forward.

As the door opens, a disgusting smell meets our nostrils. We run back into the yard.

"That's nasty!" says Kayleigh. "The guy must have left something rotting in his garbage before going out of town."

"How badly do you want to party inside?" asks Hayden. Now the rain is coming down harder.

"We can leave the door open and let it air out," I suggest. "One of us can go in and check the damage in the garbage."

"No way in hell am I checking anything that lets off that kind of stink," snorts Hayden. "I'll puke if I see anything fuzzy and squishy growing in there."

"Eww," says Kayleigh. She wiggles her head and scrunches up her shoulders, as if she could physically shake off the image. "Don't look at me for help."

As we laugh, the clouds open and rain pelts down. A lightning flash lights up the sky over the trees. We rush to the side of the house and the partial protection of the carport. The space is cramped, and the wind is blowing rain in under the roof. "Jeez, we don't usually get thunder showers this time of year," says Quinn.

"I know. The forces of nature are telling us something." I walk out into the wet air.

Kayleigh tugs on my shirt. "No, let's find somewhere else to party, please?"

"Come on, it will be fine," I say. "I'll go in and check the kitchen to see if there's spray or something that can get rid of the odour. And I'll take out the garbage."

Kayleigh lets go of my shirt and I grab the flashlight from Quinn. "But before I go in," I say, "I need something to distract me from the smell." I grab the bottle of vodka and the liquor burns my throat as it goes down. Then I plug my nose and take a deep breath as I climb onto the porch and approach the door.

I enter the dark house just as lightning brightens the sky. A boom of thunder follows close behind as the darkness takes over again. I can't hear any sounds other than the rain and my own heart thudding in my chest. I move quickly to the sink and open the cupboard under it. Sure enough, there are all kinds of cleaning supplies, including a spray bottle of Febreze. I hold it at arms' length and spray every inch of the kitchen, then aim it into the hallway.

Then I grab the garbage bin. It's full of papers and envelopes. One falls onto the floor as I tie the bag. My lungs scream for oxygen, so I run back outside and take a big breath. I drop the bag on the porch as the girls greet me with soft clapping. Quinn passes me my beer. I drink it quickly.

"Did you see anything in his house?" asks Hayden.

"Naw, I was too focused on getting the hell out before I died of stink inhalation."

Kayleigh laughs. "Well, it probably still smells. But I don't want to get soaked. Let's go in." She pulls loose the scarf that she's twirled through the belt loops on her shorts. She holds it to her nose as Hayden looks on with envy.

Quinn takes off his shirt and passes it

to Hayden so she has something to breathe through, too. She rubs her hands across his abs and smiles before placing his shirt over her mouth. As we walk up to the house, lightning cracks again. Then the sound of thunder rips through the quiet night, making Kayleigh jump.

Chapter 12

The Storm Inside

At the door, Kayleigh and Hayden stop and move off to the side. Quinn looks at me, so I enter first. Kayleigh grabs my hand just as I pass through the door and follows close behind me. Quinn and Hayden bump shoulders as they enter together. I test the air. It smells like Febreze now.

"I'm not chancing it," says Hayden as she rummages in her purse and brings out a bottle of perfume. She squirts three sprays into the air and then takes her first breath.

"I'mb breathingg through bmy bmouth," says Kayleigh.

"Where's the beer?" asks Quinn.

I realize we've left everything in the carport. I run back out and gather our drinks and snacks into my arms and snag Hayden's phone and speakers. As I turn toward the house, the sky lights up again in three quick blasts, like fireworks. Thundering booms echo back and I hear a squeal from inside.

"So, do you think it smells better?" asks Hayden, as I return to the kitchen.

"I opened the window and propped the door open. It's not a real cross-draught, but it will do," says Kayleigh.

"It's working," smiles Quinn.

"Yeah, and I think the air-conditioning came on." Hayden shivers as she passes Quinn his shirt. She opens her knapsack and pulls out a hoodie.

"Better for keeping our beer cold," I laugh. Kayleigh and I jump up onto the counter, while Hayden leans her body against Quinn's. We pass the bottle of vodka and each take a drink.

"Kitchen party. This is nice," says Kayleigh.

"I was just thinking the same thing." I smile at her. She puts her hand in mine. Then my cell rings. I know who it is without looking.

"Aren't you going to answer your phone?" asks Kayleigh.

"Nope," I say. I grab the bottle of vodka and take a deep swig. "Damn, I don't think we'll have enough booze."

"There's plenty," says Hayden, spraying the air with her perfume again.

As I count the remaining beers, Quinn asks, "Enough for Logan to drown out family stuff?"

I glare at him.

Kayleigh looks at me. "What 'stuff' is he talking about?"

Hayden pulls out her phone and rolls her

finger across the screen. She shakes her head at Quinn, showing him her calendar. "Don't go there. Not now. We're having fun."

"Will someone *please* tell me what you're talking about?" Kayleigh hops down from the counter and stands next to Hayden with her arms crossed.

"Logan, *you* tell her. It's *your* story," says Quinn.

I swig the last of my beer and slide off the counter. I grab another beer and head for the open door. I lean against the frame, my back to the kitchen.

"How much has he told you about the past?" Hayden asks Kayleigh.

"You mean past girlfriends? Not much, really," she answers.

"No, I mean about . . ." Hayden pauses.

I keep my gaze focused on the yard. But my insides boil.

Quinn finishes her sentence. "About his dad. Do you know what today is?"

"Oh, gosh. I'm sorry, sweetie," Kayleigh says, sliding in behind me. She puts one arm around my waist and is about to put her other arm there too. But I push her off and march to the centre of the kitchen. I feel my leg burn as I put pressure on it.

Kayleigh turns around. She avoids my eyes. "You don't have to talk about it."

I pace back and forth. I swig more beer. Everyone is staring at me but I don't know what to say. The lightning flashes twice and thunder booms at almost the same time. My head is like the storm, my thoughts firing like lightning, my emotions booming like thunder. Kayleigh comes to me and takes my hand. This time I let her, but my heart is still jumping in my chest.

I look at my watch. Just before midnight. "It was my dad's birthday today." I scan the room, but I don't know what for. It's as if it would be easier to share my story if I could just find the right thing to hold on to. "My dad would have been forty if my uncle hadn't . . . if Uncle Gerry would have . . ." I can't go on.

Kayleigh looks at Hayden and Quinn.

"Tell her, Quinn!" I shout, pulling my hand away from Kayleigh. "You're the one who brought it up."

Quinn puts his head down. "Sorry, dude. I was having trouble listening to your cell buzz, knowing what it was doing to you."

Hayden looks at Kayleigh. "Logan's dad and his Uncle Gerry used to go boating to celebrate their birthdays. On Logan's dad's twenty-fifth birthday, he . . ." she stumbles on the last word.

My brain erupts and I yell, "He DIED! My dad died. He's dead. Gone. And it's all my uncle's fault. *He did it*." I head toward the counter and ram my foot into a cupboard.

"Wait," says Kayleigh. "You're saying that your uncle killed your dad? His own brother? But why?"

I ignore Kayleigh's question. "He still

phones me all the time, to ask me to forgive him. Can you believe that?"

"Have you ever visited him in jail?" asks Kayleigh.

"Ah, no . . . he's not in jail." I can't meet her eyes. I can't make eye contact with any of them.

"What?" Kayleigh takes a drink from her beer can. She opens the chip bag and takes out a handful. Shaking her head she continues, "So, why is he free if he killed your dad?"

"It wasn't like that," says Quinn, pulling out a chair and sitting at the table. Hayden climbs onto his lap and puts her arms around his neck. "It was an accident."

"Then why don't you forgive him, Logan?" Kayleigh asks.

I walk back to the open door and put my head out into the damp night air. There just isn't enough oxygen. I take in deep breaths until I feel my pulse slow. But my vision is still blurred.

I turn back to face my friends. "Uncle

Gerry decided to worm his way into my life after my dad died. I was only one when I lost my father. So Uncle Gerry was like the only dad I knew. We did everything together."

"Yeah, remember that birthday with the piñata filled with candy and Lego pieces? That was . . ." starts Quinn.

I cut him off. "Like I said, he killed my dad. They were boating, and he was drinking." I feel off-balance and steady myself against the counter. Tilting my head back, I finish my beer. "My uncle had too much to drink and wasn't paying attention so he hit a bobbing deadhead. My dad went overboard. He got tangled in some netting and couldn't get up for air. Uncle Gerry panicked and turned the boat around. He didn't stop and throw my dad a life vest. No, he has to turn the boat and he ends up running over . . . he ended up stopping on top of . . . *my dad couldn't get free!*" I throw my empty beer can to the floor and stomp on it.

It flattens like road kill.

"But it doesn't sound like it was on purpose," says Kayleigh, her voice quiet. "It just sounds like . . . a horrible tragedy. It was an accident. And it seems as though he's spent his life since then trying to make it up to you. Why don't you forgive him?"

I bite my lower lip and my breath comes in short bursts. "It wasn't an accident!" I hear myself shout. "If he hadn't been drunk . . . or if they didn't go out in the boat . . ."

"Okay, not to push the issue, but what about when you were on your bike today?" asks Quinn.

I glare at him.

He continues, "What if the lady in the car had faulty brakes. Would *that* be an accident?"

I can't take it anymore. I feel like my skin is going to burst open. I brush past Quinn and storm into the hallway. I want to find a quiet spot to think. I head toward the living room. The curtains are open but it's pitch-black. I wait for my eyes to adjust to the darkness.

The sky lights up again.
Against the backdrop of light, I see him.
Then I throw up.

Chapter 13

Alone, In the Dark

The sound of me puking brings everyone running.

"KAY, STOP!" I call out. I stand on shaky legs and try to prevent her from entering the room. She looks over my outstretched arm. Hayden and Quinn run in behind us. Lightning flashes again and they see him too.

The girls scream and turn back the way they came. In seconds, I hear someone else hurling. I slump to the floor. The room is spinning. Quinn puts his hand on my shoulder and turns his head away from the grisly sight in front of us.

"Let's get out of here!" I hear Hayden cry from the kitchen.

Quinn takes several deep breaths. His fingers pinch my flesh. Then he turns on the flashlight and shines it against the wall beside us. He slowly moves it toward the centre of the living room. Toward the horrific sight in the shadows.

Old Ginger is NOT on holidays.

The stench is NOT from something rotting in the garbage.

Gingerbread Man is decomposing in his recliner.

I retch like I am going to throw up again. Quinn turns the flashlight back toward the hall. Hayden is crying in the kitchen and between sobs, she throws up. I can't hear Kayleigh at all.

Quinn extends his hand to me and I stand up.

My legs have trouble holding my weight, so I lean on him as we head back toward the other room. The smell of vomit surrounds us. Once we enter the kitchen, Hayden runs into Quinn's arms and her whole body shakes. He comforts her between sobs.

I look out to the yard. Kayleigh is standing in the rain, her head bent down. I run out to her and place my arms around her waist. She leans her head back against my shoulder. She isn't shaking. She isn't sobbing. But her body feels heavy. Like a dead weight.

"Are you okay?" I ask.

"How can I be okay? That's the first dead person I've ever seen."

I kiss her cheek. It is wet from the rain. She turns to face me. Our noses touch.

"What are we going to do now?" she asks.

"I don't know," I answer. I want to kiss her lips, but I still have a bad taste in my mouth. I pull away and take her hand to lead her back in to the house. Even as I think about protecting her from the rain, I realize I can't shield her from what is lying there, in the living room.

We climb the steps of the porch slowly. I remember the neighbours and look around. No movement. I listen for sounds of cars or people. Again, nothing but the hard drizzle of the rain.

In the kitchen, Quinn hands me a beer. He is already swigging his. I tip my head back and down the whole thing. I feel parched. My buzz is gone. I put the empty can on the counter and head to the sink. It smells of vomit. I rinse it out then grab some rags and cleaner from the cupboard. I almost step on an envelope on the floor. I pick it up and throw it onto the kitchen table.

"What are you doing?" asks Hayden with shock in her voice.

"I'm going to clean up . . . *my mess*," I answer.

"Oh, okay," she says.

"What did you think I was going to do?"

"I don't know? I thought maybe . . . I wonder if we should . . ." she stalls. Looking up at Quinn, her green eyes filled with tears, she shrugs her shoulders.

"I know what you're thinking," he says. "You are wondering if we should clean him up, or move him or something, right?"

Hayden nods, her eyes wide.

"I don't think we should touch him," says Kayleigh. "This could be a crime scene."

"That's on TV," I say. "This is real."

"That's what I mean. How do *you* think he died?" she asks.

"I didn't get a good look at him. But since he's in his chair, probably he died of a heart attack. I mean, think about it. The air conditioning is on, the newspapers are all over. I think he was home, and just died in his chair." Alone, in the dark — how else could he be here without anyone knowing he was dead? A lump forms in my throat and it's hard to swallow. "How long do you think he's been like this?"

Quinn shuffles toward the living room. "If I can stomach it, I'll try to take a look. You know I want to go into forensics. Guess I better be able to look at corpses, right?"

Kayleigh lets out a small gasp. My stomach is all twisted. It's not just what we saw in the living room. I don't know how to feel about a guy being dead and no one knowing about it.

Hayden pulls on Quinn's arm. "Don't go in there. Please, Quinn. Let's call the cops."

"It'll be okay," he says. "And we *can't* call the cops. *Remember*? We just finished breaking and entering. I want to make sure we can't be implicated in his death before we make any moves." Quinn looks at me.

Kayleigh repeats his words. "Breaking and entering?"

I can't meet her eyes. "Quinn is right. What if the cops think *we* did this?" My heart hasn't settled yet, and now it shoots into hyper-speed. I forget about cleaning up my mess.

"I'll be right back." Quinn bends down to kiss Hayden.

Kayleigh shakes her head at us. Then Hayden runs into her arms. They look at each other, then back at us.

There is a long silence. Kayleigh finally says, "Be careful."

Quinn turns on the flashlight. I follow him to the living room, but wait half in the hall. I can see the outline of Old Ginger in the glow of the flashlight, but no details. And that is fine by me.

"Logan, come hold this," says Quinn, turning the flashlight to face me.

As the light pierces my eyes I grab it with my right hand and put my left arm up to shield myself from the glare. But it is too late. All I can see are coloured spots when I blink. I move forward blindly. My sore leg bangs against a piece of furniture and I hobble sideways. Then my foot slips in something wet — probably my vomit. Losing my balance, I put my arm out to stop myself from falling. My hand grabs the recliner. Old Ginger and I would be staring straight into each other's eyes, if mine were open.

"Shit!" I stumble backward, away from the chair. Flashing the light behind me and sideways, I bump into a table and almost fall. Everything is a blur. Quinn reaches out to catch me. It takes a few moments before I can settle my breathing.

"Are you okay?" he asks.

"Yeah. I just need a minute." I slowly turn the light toward the recliner.

Chapter 14

Solving a Mystery

What we see in the chair is only half a man. It is as though his clothes are fused with his flesh. Gangly bits of thread hang around his slumped form. And as we move closer, in the thin light it looks like his tight skin is mottled orange and purple. Only his gut oozes, like something is keeping it wet.

Bones poke through in spots where the flesh is gone. And his teeth protrude out from his jaw. Spindly fingernails are hooked into the chair as though he had grabbed it hard in his last moments. Huge, vacant eyes stare at us from their sockets.

I stumble away from the chair. Quinn does the opposite. He slides toward the body. Close up like this, the stench is like sulfur and dead skunk. It burns my nostrils. "Listen, I'll be back. I just need my beer and some fresh air. Are you okay on your own?"

Quinn doesn't answer but nods his head. I leave the flashlight sitting on the edge of the table beside Old Ginger, shining so Quinn can see. I notice an empty cup and a letter on the table. As I head to the kitchen, I can hear Kayleigh and Hayden whispering.

"Would the cops really blame us?" asks Hayden. "*We* didn't do this to him. They'll be able tell he's been dead for a while, won't they?" She is drumming her nails on the table. I notice that the pattern on her nails matches her hoodie. It's like my attention has turned to body parts and I can't help noticing details.

I hobble past them to the open door and gulp in fresh air. The rain is still falling but the lightning and thunder have settled down. I grab the beers from the counter and offer them to the girls. They both decline. I take one. It is warm now, but neutralizes the taste of acid in my throat.

"What I *can* tell you," I say quietly, as I turn to face the girls, "is that this guy has been gone for some time. He's pretty decomposed. I don't know much about how these things work, but he didn't die in the last few days, or weeks, that's for sure." Even though I'm breathing, it's like my lungs are blocked and not getting any oxygen.

"How could he be dead that long? Why are we the first ones to find him?" asks Kayleigh. "You'd think his family would have called, or come by to visit."

"Remember how we said he's a loner? Maybe his family lives far away," suggests Hayden.

"How sad. No one knows he's gone. No one misses him." Kayleigh stands up from the table and comes to lean against the counter with me. She slips her hand into mine.

I think about how my uncle is a loner, too. He could die and no one would know. Except his calls would finally stop. I remember the look on his face as he stood in our doorway this afternoon — a mix of remorse and shame. I guzzle some vodka and chase it with the last of my beer.

Hayden stops strumming her fingers and slides them over the envelope I placed on the table. She picks it up and turns it in her hands. Then a look of excitement comes over her face. "Hey, I know Gingerbread Man's real name. It's right here on the outside of this envelope: Cosmos."

"Like the stars," I say.

"Sounds foreign," adds Kayleigh.

"Yeah, you're right. The address is to somewhere in Greece." Hayden looks at the envelope again. "Hang on . . ." she says.

"What?" asks Kayleigh as she joins Hayden at the table.

"Check this out. He isn't Cosmos. The letter is addressed to some lady named Mrs. Cosmos."

"Let me see," Kayleigh says, holding out her hand. Hayden passes her the envelope. "You're right. The address is to some place in Greece. But, the *return address* says 860 Dreary Lane. That's this house. He's . . ." she stutters a little as she pronounces his last name. "Mr. G. Kos-top-o-lous."

"So he didn't mail the letter?" I ask. "He wrote it, then threw it out?"

"No," sighs Kayleigh. "This letter was never opened. It's marked Return to Sender. Maybe Mrs. Cosmos doesn't live at that address, or maybe she didn't want to open the letter? Either way, it was mailed back to Mr. Kostopolous."

"Where did you get this?" Hayden asks me.

"I remember seeing it when I came in to get the garbage, it must have fallen out," I answer. Now that we know the smell wasn't coming from the garbage, I grab it from the porch and bring it in. I untie the bag. It's filled with letters all returned to Mr. K.

"Maybe we can find a clue about what happened to him," says Kayleigh, coming to stand behind me. She has a glint in her eye. She seems to have forgotten that his dead body is still rotting in the living room.

"Yeah," says Hayden. She looks interested, too. "Pass me a beer, 'kay?"

I pass her a can and open one for Kayleigh. "Whatever you do, make it quick. I'm going to take Quinn a beer," I say. "And then we've got to get out of here. I'm not doing time for a crime we didn't commit."

I leave Kayleigh and Hayden in the kitchen with the letters. I try to avoid looking at the body as I hand Quinn the last beer. "Find anything about how he died?"

"Naw," says Quinn as he opens the can and takes a swig. "I used my phone to surf the net. If the air conditioner has been on ever since he died, it would have slowed the decomposition process. He looks like pictures I've seen of mummified corpses. That's why he doesn't stink as much as you'd expect."

He smells pretty rotten to me. "So you think he may have been here for at least a month?" I ask.

"Probably," Quinn answers.

Old Ginger's rotting corpse freaks me out. "We need to figure out what we're going to do. I think we've been here too long already," I say.

Chapter 15

Too Late

"Listen to this," says Kayleigh, as Quinn and I enter the kitchen. Hayden is using her phone to create enough light to read by. "Mr. Kostopolous was writing letters to his daughter. He asks about Kalamata, the town she is living in, and about her son. Guess he has a grandkid."

Hayden pipes in, "It looks like something happened to make them disconnect from each other. He apologizes in every letter."

"But if she didn't open them, she doesn't know how he felt," says Quinn.

"Where are the cheezies?" I ask.

"Oh . . . my . . . god," says Hayden. "You can eat after seeing Mr. Gingerbread Man?"

I suddenly see his oozing gut in my mind and barely manage to keep the liquor down. Maybe eating isn't such a good idea.

"Okay, so his daughter lives in Greece. Do you think he has any family here?" asks Kayleigh. "We have to tell someone about him."

I jump in, "Maybe his phone has some numbers listed." The phone attached to the kitchen wall by the door is so old it doesn't have call display. I grab the flashlight and head to the living room. I am careful not to shine the light on Mr. K. But I can still see him from the corner of my eye.

His decaying body is worse than any zombie movie I've ever seen. I almost lose it again. I focus on the furniture. I look at the table by his recliner. No phone, but I pick up a letter sitting by the empty cup. Maybe Hayden and Kayleigh can find something interesting in it to help us solve this mystery.

I check the room at the end of the hall. It's an office. There is a phone on the desk. I scroll through the short list of saved numbers — only five names and none of them match his daughter. As I pull open a drawer, I think about how a few hours ago I considered stealing from the old guy. But finding him like this took that urge away. I close the drawer.

As I return to the kitchen, my stomach is growling for food and I taste acid again. "I'm starving. And we need to get the hell out of here."

"You're right," says Quinn. He grabs a new garbage bag and begins to pick up our chip bags and beer cans.

"But what are we going to do?" asks Hayden.

"It doesn't look like he has family here. So

we can't make a call, hoping they will come and find him and we'll be off the hook. We can't call the cops, because they'll wonder how we know about him," I say.

"This is so sad." Kayleigh is on a totally different track. "It's obvious he wanted to make amends with his daughter. But because she never opened any of the letters, she doesn't know he was ready to apologize." She lowers her voice and continues, "Don't get mad, Logan, but in a way . . ."

I know what she is going to say. She thinks this situation is the same as mine. "Hey, this is way different. My uncle actually did something that took away my dad. There's nothing in these notes to say that the guy in the living room did anything like that."

"No, but it was enough to make his daughter decide not to speak to him," says Hayden. "And now, it's too late."

Kayleigh moves the opened letters to the side of the table. "So now what?"

"For starters," says Quinn. "We erase all traces of us being here. Anything we disturbed, we need to return to its original position." He sounds like the whole season of CSI we binge watched. It was what made Quinn decide he wanted to study forensics.

"Great," says Hayden. "And what are we supposed to do with all these letters we opened?"

"They were in the trash," I reply. "We just take them with us and throw them in a bin somewhere. That was what he was going to do, anyway." I pull out the letter I found in the living room and throw it on the table. "You can add this one to the pile too."

As Quinn puts things back the way they were, I grab a cloth and cleaning supplies and head to the living room. I can hear Kayleigh reading the letter I tossed in her direction:

Dear Pappou,

I know you don't know me. Today I picked up the mail before my mom. I found your letter. I shouldn't have, but I read it. I am happy you want to meet me and want to make things better with my mom.

I am coming to Canada with my class to see the Olympic venues in Montreal, Calgary, and Vancouver. I would love to meet you when I am on the west coast. I have seen an old picture of you and we have the same eyes. I will send another note now that I have your address.

Hoping to meet you,

Evan G. Cosmos

"Logan," Kayleigh asks as I return to the kitchen. "Where did you get this letter?" She's wiping her cheeks with the back of her hand.

"It was sitting on the table . . ." I choke. "Beside him."

"He was reading this before he died? Could this be what caused him to have a heart attack?" asks Hayden.

"That sucks!" says Quinn. "That means he would have seen his grandson and could have reconnected with his daughter. But now . . ." His voice trails off.

My phone vibrates with a text message. It is after midnight, so it can't be from my mom. I open my cell to read the text. It is from Uncle Gerry.

At first I get mad. Mom must have broken her promise to me and given Uncle Gerry my cell number. He probably figures I am already asleep and won't see this until the morning.

"I'm sorry. I hope someday you can forgive me. I am going to give your dad's fishing hat to your mom. I only kept it to remind me of him. It's better if you have it. You've made it clear you don't want me in your life, and I'll respect your wishes . . ."

I don't finish reading the message. I flip my phone shut. I don't feel the burn of anger any more. I feel like I've lost something, instead.

I move closer to Kayleigh and she stands up to hug me. Her arms hold me tightly.

I look at Quinn. His arm is on Hayden's shoulder and his face is flushed. No one asks about the text and no one tells me what I should do next. I think of what Quinn said, how Mr. K's family will never know he wanted to make things right. How cruel is it that he finally has contact from his grandson, and he dies that very moment and can't answer him?

It's clear to me that Mr. K's family was broken. And now it's too late for him to fix it. If Uncle Gerry and I never repair things, will I have regrets like Mr. K?

But I don't have time to think about that

now. I take one last look around and then turn to the others. "Ready to go?" Kayleigh and I hold hands as we head to the door.

As we step outside, Quinn closes the door and locks it. He wipes around the milk chute with a cloth he grabbed from the kitchen.

Not making eye contact with Kayleigh, I take the key out of my pocket and hand it to Quinn. He wipes it down and places it in the cupboard. When I chance a look at her, Kayleigh's eyebrows are raised. I shrug my shoulders and give her a weak smile. She shakes her head, lets go of my hand, and steps off the porch. Quinn grabs the garbage bag from me, and we turn the corner into the carport.

Suddenly, we're blinded by bright lights.

A police car is sitting in the driveway.

Chapter 16

Just Like Dad

The drive from Mr. K's house to the police station is a blur. Now I'm stuck in this little cubicle by myself. Through the window, I can see Kayleigh. She's in a room just as small as mine. She doesn't look my way.

It's already light when Kayleigh's folks arrive. Her dad glares at me with a look that makes me glad there are police around to protect me. Then Hayden's parents and Quinn's dad arrive and are escorted to other rooms.

I'm still on my own. Even though it's not cold in the cubicle, my whole body shakes. Do the cops think we killed Mr. K?

While I wait for my mom, I think about how often in the past few years I've gotten away with stuff. Now that the cops have me, I might finally have to own up to some of the crap that's happened. And this time it isn't totally my fault. At least, not what happened to Mr. K.

Since no one's shown up yet, I begin to wonder if anyone's coming to help me. I'm sure Mom will arrive eventually. But I ran out on her and Uncle Gerry when she was calling me on my behaviour for the past months. I half wish that the reason my mom's late is that she's waiting for Uncle Gerry to come with her. But then I remember his text. He's done. Like I was done.

When my mom finally arrives, she's by herself. Her eyes are still dark hollows from going through yesterday alone, and now I am putting her through another ordeal. She sits down beside me. We wait in silence until an officer comes in.

"Mrs. Gomez, it appears your son is in a great deal of trouble." I wait for the officer to say we committed a murder so I can protest. But he explains, "They were caught breaking into someone's house and causing a disturbance." He turns to me as I let my breath out. Then he continues, "We found a body."

As his words fill the small room, my mom gasps and grabs the arm of her chair. Her next words come slowly, like speaking is suddenly painful for her. "Did my son . . . are you saying my son . . ."

There is a long silence before Mom gets an answer. Long enough for me to realize what she must be thinking. Long enough for me to see Kayleigh sobbing in her dad's arms. Long enough for me to wish my dad was here right now.

"No, your son did not cause this man's death."

Mom lets out the air she's been holding and loosens her grip on the chair.

The officer continues, "But these four teens used poor decision-making. They stumbled upon something they will likely never forget."

Is he ever right about that!

Before my mom can ask any more questions, he says, "Your son will have to appear in court. He will likely be sentenced to community service hours. I'll be back with more details in a few minutes." He turns to me. "Then, son, you'll have to explain what happened so we can file our report."

Silence fills the room after the officer leaves and it stays there for what seems like forever. Mom doesn't look at me and doesn't say anything. I watch out the window as Kayleigh and her parents leave. Not one of them looks my way. A few minutes later, Hayden leaves too. I wonder why only Quinn and I have to stay. Did the girls rat us out?

Kayleigh knows we found a key. Would she

and Hayden have agreed to go into the house to party if we had to jimmy the lock or break a window? I doubt it. My chest expands as I take a deep breath. I never wanted Kayleigh to be in trouble, especially since I can imagine her dad's reaction.

I stare at the peeling paint and the crooked picture on the wall, until I can't stand the silence anymore. "Mom, I didn't do the worst thing ever — that was Uncle Gerry. But I did mess up."

"You're just like your father, you know that?" she says without looking at me.

I want her next words to be about a good thing, something I did like my dad that she can be proud of. But I know that is not what she means.

Mom turns to me and puts her hand over mine. "Your father was so impulsive. He was always thinking *after* he acted. And often when it was too late. You've got his spunk," she says. A sigh escapes her mouth and hangs in the air. I feel every time I disappointed her in that single breath. "What were you thinking, Logan?"

"I wasn't, Mom. That's the problem. I wanted to escape Uncle Gerry. I wanted to escape the memories of losing Dad."

"But you never experienced losing your dad . . . not really. You were too young. If you feel loss, Logan, it's about your uncle. He's the one who picked you up when you were feeling down. He's the one who made you laugh and taught you how to ride a bike. It's your uncle who was there for every school performance when you were little. I'd crack up every Sunday when he'd arrive sporting that crazy fishing hat of your dad's. He wore it just for you, you know?"

"I didn't know that, Mom, not until a few hours ago. Why didn't you tell me the hat was Dad's?"

"Does it really matter who the hat belonged to? Your uncle wanted to make up for the father you lost — that's what matters."

I shift uncomfortably on the metal chair as anger threatens to take over again. "Don't you ever get mad?"

Mom stands up and paces the room. "Of course I do. For a long time I was angry with your father for being so careless — drinking in the boat. Letting your uncle drink. They were *both* responsible for what happened. But I came to realize that your dad died doing what he loved. Hanging out with his brother, fishing, singing in the sunshine. Yes, I'm upset that we lost him so young. But that's sadness, not anger. You have to let your anger go, Logan. It's changing who you are."

Before my twelfth birthday, I knew I'd had a dad, but I didn't miss him with this bitter pain. I loved Uncle Gerry and loved our time together. It seemed like I had everything. After I learned the truth, my anger took over. It controlled my decisions. It affected how I saw things. Even good times were seen through the red lens of anger. Now, I'm tired of feeling this way.

"But how do I forgive him, Mom? How did you forgive him?"

I'm still shivering as Mom sits beside me and puts her arm around me. I feel exhausted. I let my head rest against her shoulder.

Her voice is soft. "It will take time to forgive your uncle. Maybe you can start by making room for the good memories again."

"But you . . . how did you . . ." a giant yawn shakes my body.

"I had something more important to think about. I had you."

As her words tumble over each other in my head, sleep grabs me. I drift off.

Chapter 17

The Truth

I am startled awake when the officer bangs the door open.

"Well, son . . ." I don't like him calling me 'son'. But I let the words fall off my shoulders. I have enough to worry about. His next words could be a life sentence.

"What will happen to Logan?" Mom asks.

"That depends," the officer answers. He moves a chair in front of me and sits down. Our knees almost touch. "Think you're ready to share the truth now?"

I look at the floor. No answers there. I look at my mom. Disappointment fills her eyes. I know the answer I need to give. I know what will bring the light back to my mom's face. I take a deep breath.

"The truth is," I begin. And then the whole day comes out. From the bike ride through the red light to the moment the police catch us in Mr. K's backyard. I even tell them about the letters we found, including the one from his grandson. I can tell Mom wants to hear more about Evan and the letters. Maybe that will help us get back on track? But for now, I have to wait and see if what I shared satisfies the police.

"That seems to fit with the stories from the other three. I think you got yourselves in quite a mess last night. Seeing that man's body in the condition it's in is almost punishment enough."

"*Almost*?" I squeak.

"Almost," he repeats. "You and your

friends broke the law, and will have to do community service. Mrs. Gomez, we need you to keep close tabs on Logan for the next while. Where is his father?"

Mom chokes on her words. "Logan's father passed away when he was a baby. Now he spends a lot of time with a fellow in his twenties who is bad news." She sighs and her shoulders slump.

Mom doesn't like me hanging out with Cisco. Hell, even Quinn questions our connection. I never thought about why I started hanging with him when I did. With Cisco, I could keep on loving speed and cars like I did with my uncle. And in grade eight, Cisco became my bodyguard. Now I take care of fighting my own battles. Up until this last suspension, I thought I had that covered. But now I see how Mom thinks that Cisco has been leading me down a fast path to nowhere.

The officer continues, "You may want to find someone to help support your son.

Through the school, community members, extended family . . . It is important for a youth of his age to have a strong male role model."

"Of course," Mom answers.

I feel guilt well up in my chest and it is hard to catch my breath. Mom has always done a good job being a parent. Up until I shut Uncle Gerry out of my life, things were great. Could they be okay again? Can I fix this?

The thought of spending the rest of the summer doing community service is *not* something I'm looking forward to. But it is way better than Juvie!

✷✷✷

A couple of days later the story makes the front page of the *Peace Arch News*:

PEACE ARCH NEWS

Mr. Galenos Kostopolous, a resident of White Rock, passed away in his home. Unfortunately, his body was undiscovered for over a month. Four youth, who can't be named under the *Youth Criminal Justice* Act, have been given community service hours for breaking into his home. The police have alerted Mr. Kostopolous's next of kin.

I am glad to know that Evan and his mom have been informed. I figure this might be my ticket to talking with Kayleigh. I've given her a few days to get over things. But we still have a lot of summer to enjoy, even if part of each week will be spent doing community service.

I dial her number. I wait forever. And then I get her voicemail.

"Kayleigh. It's me. Can we talk? Are you okay? What did your parents say? Call me."

I call again four times in the next hour, but

still no answer.

I don't have to do my community service today, because I'm working at Zellers later. I'm glad, because the bus ride takes over an hour each way. Kristen, my Youth Worker from the Community Work Services Program, let me have some choice around what I could do for my placement. SUMS, the Surrey Urban Mission, seemed like a good fit and they were flexible about me keeping my job.

I hear from Quinn that Kayleigh's community work is at the drop-in community centre her dad had picked for her volunteer hours. I shower and put on my best shirt, even though it is sweltering hot outside. I want to look good.

As I ride up to the community centre, I can see kids hanging around outside. I've borrowed Quinn's bike, the one he has been using his for community service, because he was free today. His job is to clean graffiti off public walls wherever it happens.

I lean his bike against the community centre wall. It is covered in graffiti art. It's not like someone has trashed the wall, but more like people have been asked to spray paint it so it looks cool. I guess this is one wall Quinn won't have to clean.

The kids hanging around seem to be about eleven or twelve — three boys and two girls. They watch as I walk up. Kayleigh comes around the corner. She spots me, and right away turns to go back the way she came.

I run to catch up, almost twisting my ankle on a chunk of rock lying on the blacktop. "Kayleigh, wait." I catch her shoulder just before she heads inside. "Can we talk?"

She turns to face me. The mix of anger and sadness in her eyes turns my insides upside down. I stare at the ground and take a deep breath.

"I'm sorry," I begin. But she's already turned to pull open the door to the community centre. As I try to apologize again, my words bang against the door as it clicks shut in my face.

The kids hanging around outside brush past me and walk in. I follow them. Kayleigh is behind a long counter. The room has tables loaded with cards and board games. Two bean bag chairs are in one corner by a TV. The kids crash onto the couch against the wall. But they ignore the muted TV and stare at me as I approach the kitchen.

Kayleigh spreads mustard on some bread. Hayden's community service is at the Food Bank and I remember that she said some of the stuff is sent here. I watch as Kayleigh slaps meat onto the bread slices. As usual, my stomach growls at the sight of food, and the noise is loud in the quiet room. It's as though everyone is waiting to hear what I have to say. But my mouth stalls and no words come.

Kayleigh doesn't look up from the counter. She adds lettuce to the sandwiches and puts the pieces of bread together.

"Kayleigh, I don't know what to say. I just wanted to do my job, get paid and hang out with you all summer."

"Logan, I can't talk right now. I'm in major crap at home. I can't blow my community service, too. There's no telling what my dad will do."

"But . . ." I stammer.

"Hey, why don't you just back off?" One of the tweens now stands beside me. Like I am going to take that crap from a kid.

"It's okay, Sean. I can handle this," says Kayleigh.

Sean shoots a dark look my way. I ignore him and step behind the counter so I can face Kayleigh. If I can put my arms around her, she'll know how much I care. But she brushes past me into the open room.

"I don't want to see you, Logan. That's all I have to say. Go — please, just go." She disappears down a hall.

My eyes sting as I head outside. I climb

on Quinn's bike but instead of blasting down the street, my body slumps forward over the handlebars. What has changed between Kayleigh and me?

I want to get angry. How could Kayleigh treat me like this? Especially when it was my rule breaking and risk taking that she liked in the first place. But I can't find the anger in me. Maybe all this time, my anger has been covering up other feelings, like hurt. When I'm angry, I can let off steam and then things are better. But this feels like something that will never go away. And it makes my body heavy. It takes me forever to get home.

Chapter 18

Like a Mirror

"This bites," I say to Quinn as we pay for two Cokes and a bag of cheezies. It's been two days since I blew it with Kayleigh at the community centre, and I still don't know why she won't see me.

"You know she's got a right to be pissed. We got Hayden and Kayleigh in trouble with the law," says Quinn. He opens the cheezies and plops a handful in his mouth. Orange tints his fingers and lips.

I see a replay of Kayleigh's face, full of fear, as she entered the police station. "I know. But I tried to apologize."

"Maybe she doesn't need an apology."

"Okay, then what does she need?" I ask.

Quinn shrugs his shoulders.

I know I have to do something. I thank Quinn for lending me his bike again as I hop on and pedal down the street. I think about what Quinn said. Even if Kayleigh won't accept my apology, I still need to talk to her so we can sort things out. I head straight to Kayleigh's house, but her dad's car is in the driveway. I can't deal with him, so I turn back to the street and put my foot on the bike pedal. As I press down, I see the living room curtains move. Kayleigh is in the window, watching me. I'm about to wave, but her dad steps in behind her. Even through the glass, I can feel his anger reaching all the way to the sidewalk.

I take off down the street. For the first time, her dad has every right to be pissed with me. I didn't care if I got caught or not. I didn't even have those worries on my radar. Trying to stay ahead of the crap memories of the past, I've been speeding through life. And just like joyriding with Cisco, I dragged all my friends along for the ride.

Finding Mr. K is kind of like being on the wrong side of the road, street racing down the hill on 32nd Avenue and hitting a car coming straight for us. And now I have to wonder if Kayleigh and I are really over, like the damage after a crash?

With Cisco, I never have to face things. And I've been giving Kayleigh and Quinn attitude each time they tried to help me deal with my feelings. Maybe it's time I chilled and started to listen.

For the next two weeks, I think about Kayleigh every day. I can't summon the courage to call her or to go see her at the community centre. And I am busy with work at Zellers and my community service at SUMS. I'm on the bus to North Surrey when I get a call from Cisco.

"What's your deal?" he asks.

"Ah, nothing. On my way to SUMS."

"Right, community service," he says. "When are you done?"

"About three more weeks, I think." A woman gives me a dirty look for talking on my cell phone.

"No, I mean, how long is your shift today?"

"Oh," I say. "Until seven. Why?"

"Cuz we're on, dude!"

"Crap. You mean the guy with the Mazda — he's ready to race?" I lower my voice to be sure no one hears me.

"Yup! Tonight — I'll pick you up when you're finished your shift."

"Cool," I say. Then I sigh. "No, wait. I can't." If I get caught street racing I could be facing *real* time. And like Quinn, I want to make it to twenty. "I can't risk it. I've got community service to finish and Kayleigh . . . I just can't. Not now. Not . . ." my voice trails off.

"I hear ya, kid. Next time, then!"

I click my phone shut and look out the window.

I really screwed things up. Even if I don't street race, all I do when I hang with Cisco is drown my stress in alcohol. And though I feel like I could use a drink right now, brown-bagging it on a city bus on my way to do community service is crazy. I give my head a shake.

I jump off the bus at my stop, then hike the four blocks to SUMS. I actually like working here. But I didn't bargain on cutting so many onions. I've been crying like a baby for two weeks. I have helped sort through donated clothes (some are pretty nice-looking too), but they've mostly kept me busy in the kitchen. I was surprised to find I like food prep, even peeling onions. My supervisor Mike tells me that it's something I could look into after I finish school.

Mike asks me to take some fruit out to the main dining area. So far, all the people I've seen coming through SUMS have been adults — mostly older adults. I've talked with this one guy almost every time I volunteer. He's totally into vinyl and car races. It's almost like it used to be spending time with Uncle Gerry.

I bring the fruit out to the folks eating their supper. Then I stop dead, like I've been shocked by a taser. I whip around and brush past Mike, practically knocking him over. "Hey, what gives?" he asks as I retreat to the kitchen. I peek through the window out to the main dining area, where a young guy is standing in line waiting to get food.

It's like I'm looking in a mirror. His hair is the same colour as mine, but it's longer and hides half his face. He's about my age. When I first started at SUMS, Mike said I'd see people of all ages. I thought he meant adults. I never expected to see someone in their teens.

I take the garbage out back so I can avoid the guy I just saw. Mike follows me.

"Are you okay?" he asks.

"I was just surprised, that's all. It's like that young guy in the line could be me, except he has no home or food. What's his story? Did he ditch his family? Did they ditch him?" Now that we're talking, my heart kicks down a notch.

"I can't tell you why he's here — that's confidential. But young people like him do come in. They are one of the reasons I do this work. It's important for people to have someone looking out for them. Someone who cares about what happens to them."

I think about my mom. It's not like we'll be on the streets in the next month. But money is always tight and we have to watch what we spend. What if we couldn't pay the bills? Or the rent? I was supposed to be helping my mom, looking out for her. But instead I've been throwing cash around like we're loaded.

Mike continues, "Do you have someone like that in your life, Logan?"

"I . . . yeah. My mom, I guess. And . . ." I run my fingers through my hair and kick at the loose gravel by the garbage bin. I don't have Kayleigh anymore. And now, because of me, my mom doesn't have Uncle Gerry.

Still, compared to the guy in the line, I am pretty lucky. At least I'm on the other side of the counter — even if it is for all the wrong reasons.

"Hey," I say to Mike, "I'm sorry I bumped into you like that. I plan on working hard from now on." I want to put some distance between my own life and the nameless teen eating a bowl of chili at SUMS.

"It's all good," says Mike. "You've kept your head down and you get the work done. I've noticed you talking with Charlie. He tells me you like old records too. He enjoys your company. Opening up to the people we help here enriches our lives, as much as it improves their lives." I nod in agreement and get back to work.

When I'm done for the day, I head home. I do the dishes and look at the vegetables in the fridge. Mom always comes home tired from work, so I decide it's time for me to help out more. While I cut mushrooms for spaghetti sauce — and still more onions — I think about the Sunday dinners we could make together. In my mind, I see my mom laughing as Uncle Gerry tries to roll burritos without slopping the filling all over the counter.

True to his text, Uncle Gerry hasn't called once since my dad's birthday. I figured that would make me happy. But happy isn't what I'm feeling now.

Chapter 19

Letting Go

Quinn comes over Friday afternoon. At first I thought community service would mean working for free from nine to five. Every day. But we both have the day off, even though we still have more time to serve.

"So, Kayleigh and Hayden finished their community service hours," says Quinn as he flops down onto the couch. "I guess Kayleigh's dad used his influence, or money, to make sure they had lighter sentences. Funny thing is,

Kayleigh has decided to stay on at the centre. She says she loves it there."

"Wow." I still can't get used to thinking of Kayleigh being out of my life. Hearing her name makes my heart race. "She seems pretty good at it too," I answer. "She already had one of the teens defending her the day I went to apologize."

"Have you heard from her yet?"

"Naw. And I don't think I will." I shuffle back and forth on my feet. Sounds of a car race blare from the TV. I wouldn't mind hitting the road, fast like that. I see now that running and racing have always been my MO.

As Quinn fiddles with the remote, the feeling of needing to move gets stronger. I have to do something with this restlessness inside me. "So, my mom got me a used bike from a co-worker," I tell Quinn. "How about going for a ride? Maybe fly down Oxford Street like we used to? I need to get out of my head."

"Sure, but let's grab lunch first," adds Quinn.

We head to the A&W off King George. It is a long ride and, even though we aren't going fast, the pedalling still makes me feel better. As we enter the restaurant, I see Kayleigh sitting with Hayden. Her back is to the door so she doesn't see us come in. But Hayden does. She starts to wave at Quinn but puts her hand down as soon as she realizes that I'm with him. She whispers something to Kayleigh, then nods our way.

Kayleigh brushes past me in her haste to get out the door. Quinn sits down with Hayden as I follow Kayleigh out onto the sidewalk. She paces and chews her nail.

"I'm not here to pressure you. I didn't know you would be at the restaurant. Quinn was hungry," I say.

Her black hair is shining in the sunlight and her blue eyes glisten. I want to take her hand. I move a step forward, and then retreat. "I hear you like the community centre and you're going to keep working there. That's awesome — the kids obviously love you. I mean, who wouldn't?"

"Logan, you . . ." She turns to look at me. Her eyes are wide and tears line her lower lid. "Look, I'm sorry I couldn't talk to you before. I was just too angry . . . and humiliated."

"I know. I'm sorry I put you through all of this."

"You don't need to apologize."

Kayleigh's words don't make any more sense to me than they did when they came out of Quinn's mouth before.

She continues, "You didn't make me go into Mr. K's house."

"Yeah, we pressured you and Hayden," I say.

Kayleigh moves to one of the concrete picnic tables outside the restaurant and plops down. I sit across from her. I can see Quinn and Hayden inside, staring at us.

"No," she continues. "We made our own choices. It took me a while to realize why I was so mad at you. At first I was angry because I had to face the wrath of my father, alone. I was upset that I shamed my family. I rag on my dad all the time, and I admit, I liked seeing him get worked up over you. But, I never meant to embarrass him." She leans her head on one hand. "Now I realize how immature it was of me to be striking out at my dad. I see that I should have been making better decisions about my own life. I've been doing a lot of thinking."

"Me too!" I say. "I never meant for all this to happen."

"But it did happen, Logan. Do you know that juvenile offenders don't normally get community centres to make up their service time? I only got this gig because of my dad — because I had already applied to volunteer there. I had to convince the supervisor at the community centre and my Youth Worker that I had made a terrible mistake." She sighs. "It's hard to shake this off. It's real and we screwed up."

"*You* didn't screw up. *I* did. I didn't care what kind of trouble I was getting into. And I didn't care who else would be hurt when I brought all of you along. I just wanted to get rid of the memories so I wouldn't have to deal with my feelings."

"But you can't erase your memories. They are part of who you are. Quinn told me about the times you spent with your uncle. Logan, you have to hang onto all your memories, the good ones and the bad ones."

I lower my voice and my stomach rumbles. This time it's not from hunger, but from guilt. "I had a lot of anger, and I didn't know what to do with it. The only time I felt free of it was when I did reckless things. Then I was flying high on adrenaline. But it was a mistake to get my friends involved. The last thing I wanted was to make your life harder. Mine sucks, but I didn't mean to make yours that way too."

"Do you really believe your life sucks?"

"Yeah. No. When you were in it — it was good."

She smiles. "What about when your uncle was a part of your life? Before you knew he made a terrible mistake?"

Her words hit home. "That's it, isn't it? He made a mistake." As I say the words, I know she's right. "Uncle Gerry's been trying to apologize for years and I wouldn't listen. But, Kayleigh, what if it's too late? What if I can't forgive him? What if I can't love him again?"

Forgiveness and love. That's what I've been wanting from Kayleigh these past weeks. And not getting them has been driving me crazy. It's hard to forgive someone when you're stuck in anger. But Kayleigh let me talk after only a couple of tries. I've spent four years being angry with Uncle Gerry.

She turns and looks inside the restaurant where Hayden and Quinn are still watching us. I have to smile. I realize what good friends they are, and how much they care about what happens to us.

She slides her hand over mine.

"Does this mean you forgive me?" I ask.

There's a pause and then Kayleigh says, "It's not me you should be asking forgiveness from."

Epilogue

At the end of the summer, I invite Kayleigh for a picnic at Harrison Lake. We pile into the car, even my mom. She has to drive with us to the lake, because of my learner's permit. Once we arrive in Harrison, Mom goes shopping along the main street near the Hot Springs Hotel while Kayleigh and I have lunch. On our way to the far end of the beach, I show Kayleigh the spots Uncle Gerry used to share with me.

We spread out our blanket and open our

picnic lunch. Kayleigh has made potato salad and coleslaw, and I brought chicken.

"Before we eat, I want to say something," I begin. "I spent a lot of time thinking about what you said to me outside the A&W. I finally figured out who it is I need to forgive. I need to forgive myself for feeling like I betrayed my dad by letting Uncle Gerry into my life. I need to forgive myself for wasting four years hating him."

Kayleigh eats some potato salad and chases it down with a swig of iced tea. Then she says, "I've done some thinking too, Logan. At first I took that dare to go out with you because of your hot looks and your bad-boy image. You know, the danger — the excitement. I'm not even sure when things shifted, but I started to care for the *real* you — not the image, but the person. Does that make sense?" I nod and she goes on, "The scene with Mr. K was all about danger and excitement, until it backfired. You said it was your fault. But it wasn't. I chose to go into Mr. K's house to party. You chose to break in and not tell me. And boy, did our choices have consequences."

Her words bounce around in my head with the ones my mom shared at the police station. All this time, I've been blaming Uncle Gerry for my dad's death. But my dad chose to go in the boat with him. He chose to drink and to let his brother drive the boat when he'd been drinking. Okay, my dad didn't choose to die that day, but now I see how Uncle Gerry didn't mean for things to turn out the way they did.

"I get it," I say out loud. "I wish I could change the past. But I can't. What I can control is how I feel about it. Up until now, I've chosen anger. And really, I didn't care about what happened to me." I look up and Kayleigh is nodding her head. I continue, "But I do care about what happens to you."

"I didn't realize how much I care about how the things *I do* affect other people," says Kayleigh. "I've always loved rebelling against my dad. But these past weeks, when he isn't yelling at me, I've seen the look in his eyes. Sadness I caused by being careless. Do you know something? That's been harder to deal with than when he and I were fighting all the time."

"What a summer, hey?" I say, as I bite into a piece of chicken. When I take a spoonful of coleslaw, some of the dressing slops down my chin. Before I can wipe it away with the back of my hand, Kayleigh is cleaning it off and leaning in to kiss me. She wraps her arms around me, and it's back like it always is when we're together. We stay that way for a long time. When we finally come up for air, my stomach is growling for more food. Together, Kayleigh and I finish every bite of our lunch.

After the picnic we drive Kayleigh home. Then we stop at the park so Mom and I can talk.

"Thanks, Mom, for riding along to Harrison. I can't wait until I graduate to an N."

"I can wait! You are growing up too fast." She pats my knee. We're sitting on a bench, watching kids play with their parents.

I take a deep breath and crack my knuckles before saying my next words. "Mom, I want to thank you for not blowing up at me when we were at the police station. You could have added extra time for me to do at home. Or you could have just given up on me. But you didn't. How come?"

"I could see you were struggling, Logan. After you stopped seeing your Uncle, you changed. You were angry all the time, and then you began drinking. Once you started hanging out with Cisco, you let him drag you into doing some pretty reckless things. It was almost as though you wanted to get caught — to be punished — but I couldn't understand for what."

"Maybe I was punishing myself for betraying Dad. For loving Uncle Gerry all those years. When I found out he took Dad away from us, things flipped. Being angry with him was kind of like my way of making it up to Dad. But that totally failed."

Mom turns to face me. "I was so worried about you. I'm one of the reasons your uncle kept calling. I asked him to. I knew you needed someone, and I knew you meant the world to him. I believe it was your uncle's way of making amends to your dad. Being there for you, since your dad couldn't be."

My eyes catch a grandpa pushing his young grandson on the swings. I think of Mr. K and Evan. I think of the police officer, calling me 'son'. I miss Uncle Gerry calling me *Mi hijo*.

"Well, I am working on things. I still get angry, but I'm better at controlling it." I think about the past few weeks. I've fought the urge to grab a bottle of liquor every time I'm pissed at the world. "And guess what? Like you suggested, I've been remembering some of the good times I had with Uncle Gerry. Especially our plans to see the Baja 1000."

"You were thinking of going to Mexico?"

If I'd kept the relationship with Uncle Gerry we would be booking tickets to Mexico for November. I've lost a lot of time holding on to resentment. My shoulders slump. Mom slides closer to me.

"Yeah," I say. "We both loved fast things. But it's too late now. He's done, right?"

Mom brushes a loose strand of hair from my face. She says, "With people you love, it's never too late."

I decide to stay at the park as Mom heads home. I watch the kids play and think about boat rides and birthdays. I remember how Uncle Gerry was pissed when his favourite Mexican restaurant closed down at the pier. My mom found a new one in Langley by her work. I wonder if he knows about it? I think about the race and how Uncle Gerry used to say he'd teach me Spanish, that I'd need it when we went to Mexico.

After an hour, I'm still not ready to go home. I decide to call Mom to let her know I'll be late for dinner, but my fingers tap out Uncle Gerry's number.

I don't hang up. Instead, I hold my breath and wait to see if he will answer.

Acknowledgements

With much gratitude to the folks at Pacific Community Resources Society who helped me understand community work service in Surrey, and to Dr. Gail S. Anderson, Professor in the School of Criminology at SFU. Dr. Anderson helped me with forensic questions while she was on holidays! Writers rely on research and it is wonderful to find so many supportive people in the community.

Also, heartfelt thanks to Kat, my editor, who saw the potential in this story and helped the novel find its way. It is a treat to work with you. Thanks again to my mom and dad for their tireless support of my writing efforts!